HEATHER BOYD

USA TODAY BESTSELLING AUTHOR

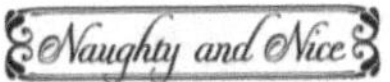

Naughty and Nice

In the Widow's Bed

Naughty and Nice Series in print

One Wicked Night and other short
stories
In the Widow's Bed
Love Me Tender
Love Me True
A Husband for Mary
Let It Snow

DEDICATION

For my darling beloved for having faith that writing wasn't simply a passing fancy.

CHAPTER ONE

Berkshire, England
1814

IF EVER A GENTLEMAN stood in need of forbearance then this confounded house party surely fit the bill. Jonathan Oliver, Earl of Selwood, stood amid the giddy throng and wished himself a thousand miles away. The perfumed stench of his best friend's circle of acquaintances—each resplendent in more silk, satin, and sparkling jewels than necessary—choked the very breath from his lungs.

He eased out of the mind-numbingly boring conversation he'd become trapped in and moved away in search of more appealing quarry. Unfortunately, a hand clamped over his upper arm before he'd gone very far.

"I tell you, she's up to no good, Selwood."

Jonathan groaned but turned to face his friend, Lord Warminster. A man who was never entirely what he seemed. "To whom do you refer to *this* time?"

Warminster's fingers tightened. "Lady Warminster, of course."

Jonathan glanced down at the hand that held him in place. "How so?"

Warminster released his arm. "Her whole face lights up whenever any gentleman comes into view, has done so all evening too. Can you not see what I mean?"

Jonathan saw nothing in Lady Warminster's manner to precipitate such a high level of distrust. But then again, he was conversing with the most suspicious man in England and should hardly be surprised by the direction of his friend's thoughts.

Warminster's stepmother, widowed these last four years, glided past with a group of twittering acquaintances. Her deeper, earthy chuckle reached Jonathan's ears as she clung to his sister's arm, sharing a confidence.

The lady appeared to him as she always had. Utterly breathtaking. He could see nothing wrong with her behavior.

"If anything, your mother appears happy," Jonathan conceded. "About time." He muttered the last under his breath, knowing his older friend would likely not agree.

Beside him, Warminster's scowl deepened. "Step mother."

A servant passed them with a tray of champagne and Jonathan's friend scooped up a glass with an extravagant movement, downed the contents whole, and then returned the empty glass to the tray. "I have a job for you, Selwood."

"No!" Jonathan groaned. Whenever Warminster needed something done, no matter how innocuous the matter sounded at first hearing, Jonathan would certainly face a moral dilemma by the end. He didn't like to spy on acquaintances, but Warminster often called on him to do so whenever he had state business elsewhere. And his request couldn't possibly come at a more inconvenient time.

"I need you to keep an eye on her," Warminster said. "With the house so full of guests, I cannot watch over her closely enough."

Damn Warminster to hell and back. Jonathan had plans for this house party. Watching over an unattainable woman wasn't high on his list. His mind was set—fixed—on what he *could* get his hands on. "She's a grown woman. Let her have a bit of fun for a change if she wants it. Good God, why must you meddle constantly?"

"Because—" Warminster groaned dramatically—"it appears to me that my dear step mother is intent on flinging away her mourning for my father only to throw herself into some scoundrel's arms. It is imperative she not form inappropriate—and potentially inquisitive—romantic attachments. I do not need this right now."

Jonathan turned his gaze to Lady Warminster and he stared. Conducting an affair with the lovely widow was an opportunity no man would turn down. "She'd hardly do what you fear," Jonathan whispered, breath lost as his pulse beat a sudden gallop.

"Look at her. The clothes, the jewels, the elaborate hair fashion." Warminster's glance darted left and right. "Damn it, Selwood, she even commissioned a new scent. I can see a mad scheme as well as anyone."

Mad scheme or not Phoebe Torrington, Lady Warminster, could tempt any man to consider a dalliance. She might be ten years Jonathan's senior, but she moved as sensuously as a much younger woman. Her head lifted and then turned in their direction. Pale green eyes held his gaze across the ballroom floor, and her lips curved upward in a polite smile. To his way of thinking, she had done nothing new to encourage a pleasure-hungry bachelor. She didn't seem a lady in search of a willing bedfellow at all. He couldn't imagine her throwing propriety aside at any time.

But Lord Warminster had to be dissuaded from including him in this bit of folly. "I'm not staying for the house party. How exactly do you expect me to accomplish this feat?"

His arm was grasped firmly, and they moved them further into the room. "Actually, you are. I had your things brought over earlier tonight. Just look at the image she presents. She's smiling too damn much. She cannot take Plimms for a lover. He's riddled with the bloody pox."

Jonathan let his eyes linger on Lady Warminster again—sleek, supple, and widowed far too young—the golden beauty deserved better than to suffer for her first choice of lover after becoming a widow, if that's what she intended. "I'm sure you're mistaken."

"I'm not. I never am." Warminster flashed his rings before him and made a show of admiring the pieces. "I don't have that luxury. I cannot interfere in her life now. I've done everything I can to keep her apart from my life so she faced no danger."

Jonathan examined his friend closely. Pale,

elaborately curled hair and foppish attire hid a man capable of committing unspeakable acts in the defense of his country. The danger to Lady Warminster had once been all too real. His friend had divided the family and rarely saw them to keep up the charade. The carefree demeanor he had adopted in society concealed his real profession from acquaintances remarkably well.

Jonathan was one of the few to be told the truth, and he had never found Warminster's intelligence wrong. Not yet at any rate. And if that was so then Lady Warminster was ripe for an affair—with the right man of course. He let out a harsh breath, groaning at his inevitable compliance. "Fine, fine." He tugged on his dark spotted waistcoat, a dull affair when compared with his friend's gold-stitched finery. "Where have you put me?"

Warminster's face creased into a beatific smile. "Why, in the last room available, of course. Next to hers in the family wing."

Jonathan coughed to cover his shock. "It's not like you to be so obvious. She will discover you've set me to watch her."

"Lady Warminster isn't a fool by any means. All you have to do is get between her and her would-be swains." Warminster's jaw clenched for a moment, but then he seemed to remember the role he had to play and replaced it with a carefree grin.

No matter how much he wished it, Warminster wouldn't change his mind. But if Jonathan disagreed then his friend would conscript half the servants to watch the lady for the remainder of the evening, and the remaining days of the house party. That situation didn't sound particularly enjoyable for her.

Perhaps he could prevent the lady from meeting with a lover of *her* choice. Since they got along well, she might even listen to his warnings and let *him* do the choosing. The thought brought a wicked image to mind. Jonathan quashed it. Had he forgotten what he was really here for so quickly?

Jonathan scanned the room again, but his quarry was nowhere to be seen. Again. His future wife must have retired already so he had ample time to investigate Warminster's ridiculous idea before he *had* to act the charming suitor.

Warminster stirred beside him. "Now you've agreed—and I can see you have—I'll leave you to your duties. Make sure she remains above reproach. I don't care how many scoundrels you have to kick away from her door just keep her unentangled."

With a slap to Jonathan's shoulder,

Warminster moved away but stopped at a cluster of merry guests to join in their discussion with great enthusiasm. That false charm he employed so vigorously got under Jonathan's skin at times, but at least the opinions Lord Warminster sprouted so often to others were nowhere near what the man himself believed.

Wondering at the strange turn of events, Jonathan prowled the stifling ballroom, nodding to acquaintances while keeping Lady Warminster in view. She stood in a cluster of giggling females and, as long as she remained there, he didn't have cause to be concerned. It was only if she left them on her own that he would need to keep watch. Sure that all was in order for the time being, he turned for the refreshment table and a much needed brandy.

"Why are you skulking about, Selwood?"

Jonathan turned to find his sister hovering at his elbow. "I do not skulk."

Lizzy uttered an inelegant snort as she brushed an escaping lock of dark hair behind her ear. "Then this is the finest display of not skulking you have ever done. Are you vexed because Warminster claimed a first dance with Lady Jocelyn before you had a chance to even ask?"

Jonathan scowled. Wonderful. He and his friend had chosen the same chit to woo. Had

Warminster sent him off on a fool's errand so he might have a clear field? Possibly. He couldn't see them yet, but he wouldn't be outwitted by an overdressed popinjay. The night was still young.

Jonathan tucked Lizzy's arm through his and started a slow circuit of the room, hoping to find Lady Jocelyn. "And what is to account for your prickly demeanor this evening? Has someone had the gall to suggest you might stand up with them for a set?"

Lizzy looked about them with such obvious disdain that he laughed.

"A greater bunch of numbskulls couldn't exist in one place again. Is Warminster acquainted with anyone in possession of more than a feather of intellect in his brain?" She raised her free hand before he could respond. "No, don't answer that. You'll only protest his supposed intelligence. I'd rather not argue with you about your choice of friends again. By the way, you should congratulate me. My plan for a singular future is well underway. I've barely had to refuse a dance all evening."

He skirted a trio of fluttering debutants, keeping Lizzy between him and their attempts at flirtation. She was correct in her assessment of Warminster's guests, a gaggle of numbskulls indeed. Except for Lady Jocelyn, of course. She seemed very promising. "I cannot imagine why the notion of marriage so disgusts you," he said.

Lizzy dug her heels in. "Well, you're a fine one to talk. The day you consent to undertake matrimony is the day I might do the same. Lucky for me that day will come when my hair has altered to the brightest silver for I cannot imagine the fastidious Lord Selwood married."

The same argument. Another venue. He wasn't as fastidious as his sister claimed. He just required a certain level of intelligence in a woman. Associating with Lord Warminster's set had not thrown such women into his path until the pretty Lady Jocelyn had come out this spring and appeared a likely candidate for a wife. Like his sister, he required intelligence in a potential spouse. Yet, as Jonathan looked about them, he wondered if there was anyone here he could encourage to pursue Lizzy.

Not Peters. Or Ridgeway. Perkins was an amiable chap. He'd have to have a word later and see if he couldn't be encouraged to consider her in a favorable light. Then he could work on softening Lizzy to the idea. How did one disembark one's sister from the family home when she was dead set against the happy union of marriage? The way things were going, she'd still be joining him for breakfast on the day he died.

"Oh, bother—" Lizzy slouched. "—now *he* is

a persistent numbskull. Mr. Perkins is coming this way again. If he keeps this up I'll have to geld him to keep him at bay. Why will he not take a hint? *Au revoir*, Selwood."

"Bonne chance, enfant!"

With a stubborn glare for her pursuer, Jonathan's long-legged sister bolted from the ballroom. Perkins craned his neck to watch her flight, and he did appear to consider setting out in pursuit, but then he shrugged and limped to a chair, snatched up a glass of champagne from a passing footman, and settled into the cushions.

Why would any gentleman in his right mind seriously consider Lizzy, with her coltish charms, a candidate for matrimonial felicity? She'd be likely to conk the poor gent on the head before the wedding night started.

Depressed, Jonathan accepted Lizzy's continued presence at his breakfast table for as long as they both shall live.

"Why so great a sigh, Lord Selwood?" Lady Warminster murmured at his side. "Are you searching for a dance partner and unable to catch the lady's eye?"

Jonathan spun, an honest smile lifting his lips. "I was considering it. Would you care to dance with me, Lady Warminster?"

"But of course." Her eyes sparkled with humor. "I know you to be a fine dancer, so I have no fear for my toes."

Jonathan dropped his gaze to the lower edge of her gown. "Such delicate toes. Have they been much trodden on this evening?"

"Perhaps." She glanced around. "I believe the last waltz of the night is about to play."

"Perfectly timed then, my lady." He drew her arm through his. Delicious warmth dragged a deep-seated need to the surface. Her scent—violets if he was not mistaken— lured him to lean close. But true to her words, when the current set ended, the orchestra announced a waltz with a short violin piece. Fate was certainly favoring him this evening with regard to one woman.

Lady Warminster settled into his arms and flowed with him into the dance. Despite the fatigue often displayed at this late hour, she moved lightly, perfectly pliant as they swirled around the polished parquetry. "How has your evening progressed?"

"Oh, as well as ever."

Jonathan glanced down at her face. Her gaze drifted over his left shoulder, examining the crowd lining the floor. After a few turns he inched her closer, pulling her deeper into his embrace until her gaze rose to meet his. "You appear to be searching for someone, my lady?"

Her face pinked and her gaze fell to his chest. "No. No, of course not."

With Lady Warminster pressed closer against his body, he could see why her stepson held concerns. The plump curves of her breasts made Jonathan's mouth water. Any gentlemen would risk scandal to sample the view this daring new gown displayed.

"Liar," he whispered as her gaze flickered over his shoulder again to the crowd lining the dance floor. "Your attention has wandered from me already. The other gentlemen have surely noticed. Most embarrassing."

Lord Plimms circled the ballroom floor in puce satin, his gaze lingering—if he wasn't mistaken—on the shift of fabric over Lady Warminster's rump. Jonathan maneuvered them further away.

She glanced up. "Whatever do you mean?"

He snorted. "If a lover is what you seek you could do better than inviting Plimms to your bed. The man is certainly poxed."

Lady Warminster's cheeks colored a deeper red. "I wasn't considering him. Not really."

"Good. There are far more worthy men you should consider for the honor ahead of Plimms."

Jonathan let the silence lengthen then drew to a halt when the dance ended. He bowed over her hand, but tucked Lady Warminster's arm through his to lead her from the floor, avoiding the lurking gentleman. Plimms appeared ready to approach, but Jonathan scowled and changed course through the crowd until the reforming dance lines stood between them.

When they stopped, Lady Warminster slipped from his grasp. "You surprise me, my lord. I shouldn't expect you'd approve of such a decision. Not with you being Warminster's closest friend."

He grinned but didn't answer.

"Ah, I see." Her mouth twisted as if she'd tasted lemons. "The giggling fop sent you to dissuade me, didn't he?"

Jonathan laughed outright. "What your son sent me to do—and what I intend—is quite another matter." He linked her arm through his again and they strolled along the edge of the ballroom.

Lady Warminster settled her hand on his sleeve. "Do you think me foolish?"

Jonathan found an empty corner and settled them onto a vacant chaise. "I believe you're brave to risk upsetting Warminster."

She rolled her eyes. "He might hold the title now, but he's still my son. I know exactly what he's about with his charade."

Jonathan absorbed her remark. He'd had a suspicion Lady Warminster had discovered her stepson's private activities. But he had to tread carefully. The matter wasn't his to discuss openly. "He's intent on protecting you."

She brushed at a pale curl, one newly escaped from her elegant coiffure. Jonathan itched to set the remaining mass free. "Not even his father behaved with such managing control," she said.

Jonathan settled deeper into the cushions. He really didn't want to discuss her late husband—a man many years her senior when she'd married him—or whether she missed or did not miss him. He'd rather discuss her intention to take a lover. "What is it you want, my lady?"

"To make my own choices," she whispered.

He patted her hand. "If choosing Plimms was your choice then I fear you might need some guidance."

Lady Warminster stared out at the sea of swirling revelers. At first, he didn't think she'd continue their conversation, but then she took a deep breath, forcing her breasts higher in the gown. "What would you suggest?"

Perfect! He smothered a grin. "I believe you should lay down some guidelines for your lover."

She turned. "Such as?"

Her pale green gaze fastened on him, kicking his pulse higher. To hide his unsettled state, he offered a lopsided grin. "Well, if it were me, I'd pick clean as a first condition."

She blinked and looked about them, discreetly checking that they were not being overheard. "And is that easy to discern?"

Her delicate hand landed on the cushion beside his thigh. Just one more inch and she'd have touched him. "Not always. That's why I'm offering my insights. Gentlemen do gossip." Jonathan shifted his leg until the material of his dark breeches brushed her fingers.

"Ah, I had surmised as much already." Lady Warminster withdrew her hand. "Warminster's tongue *is* hinged in the middle." She focused on the dance floor again. "Tell me about the men here."

Eager for an excuse to touch her again, he climbed to his feet then held out his hand. "Let's walk for a bit. We're drawing attention."

As Lady Warminster slipped her small gloved hand into his, Jonathan tugged her to her feet. They were mere inches apart when her gaze rose to meet his, but he managed to behave and hold out his arm. The temptation to act improperly grew as she licked her lips before curling her arm about his. He guided her through the ballroom, away from any friends' curious glances.

When they arrived at a less crowded spot,

he leaned close to her again. "I assume you also want a man of considerable skill to, ah—" he searched for the right word—"dance with you?"

"That is what I hope," she whispered.

Her timid admission dragged another bubbling laugh from his chest. "That should be the whole point. Hmm, there are few suitable gentlemen to choose from at your son's house party. But there are men here who would pleasure you in a chamber lit to brilliance and still proclaim you the brightest star."

At Lady Warminster's shocked gasp, Jonathan led her out onto the terrace where darkness hid her embarrassment from any witnesses. "Or would you prefer the comfort of darkness for your daring escapade?"

He drew closer, slid the tips of his fingers along her arm, over the thin strip of skin exposed to the night between her glove and gown to gauge her reaction. She shuddered, her hitched breath loud in the dark night. Unfortunately, his body reacted too. Her velvet skin stirred a hunger in him he strove to control. "You prefer the darkness, I think." Lady Warminster didn't answer, but she didn't move away from his fingers. Jonathan smiled and continued to caress her. "Darkness can be delightful too."

"You're trying to make me feel better. How

very like you." Her wine-sweet breath brushed his jaw, and Jonathan's pulse hammered erratically through his body.

"I aim to please." Reluctantly, he increased the space between them so anyone stumbling onto the terrace wouldn't suspect their conversation as anything but polite chatter between friends. He also needed time to master his body before he was fit to be seen. "So, clean, skilled in the bedroom, and not averse to a clandestine tryst. Is there anything else you want from your lover, madam?"

"Yes, absolute discretion," she said firmly. "I don't want anyone else to hear of it."

CHAPTER TWO

LORD SELWOOD'S sigh rattled Phoebe's strained composure. She was already pushing the boundaries of propriety by discussing such a personal matter with her stepson's bachelor friend. The young man must be positively astonished to hear a woman her age speak of taking a lover so candidly. She was two and thirty years old but there had always been something in Selwood's manner that encouraged her to share confidences with him. He couldn't be more different than her stepson—a man so steeped in his double life as a spy that even his secrets had secrets.

Where Warminster frittered and gossiped about anything of no importance to hide what he was likely doing, Selwood held his tongue about everything. Unfortunately, his physical presence had quite the wrong effect on her nerves. She'd never met a man—and so young a man at that—who rattled her senses the way he did. One glance from his dark eyes made her long for the intimacies of the bedchamber, no matter her location.

Her reaction to him ensured she simply couldn't pretend to be satisfied with the life of enduring mourning. So despite the likely difficulty, she'd set herself the task of finding a lover this summer.

Luckily, Selwood had no idea how she struggled to keep her composure around him. It simply could not be decent for a woman her age to stir with lust for a man ten years her junior.

"Secrecy makes your desire a little harder to accommodate. But not impossible." Selwood mused. "However, there might be one particular gentleman who should be agreeable and willing to meet with you at short notice. I assume you'd like something arranged for this evening?"

Phoebe let out the breath. Despite how wicked the conversation, she was excited. At least Selwood didn't consider her desire impossible to accommodate. How had she thought to encourage a man—the right man—without his insights? "Thank you."

The young man's gaze burned with a strange intensity, but then he glanced away, shuffling restlessly. "We should return to the ballroom soon, but are you certain you want such a secretive arrangement? You might never discover whom I send to you."

"I trust you." And she did. Of all Warminster's friends, Lord Selwood's serious nature set her mind at ease. His friendly presence, his obvious esteem had proven she placed her trust in the right gentleman. It was simply her problem to hide that she desired him.

Selwood offered a little bow. "I'm honored."

Despite the pleasant civility, Phoebe chuckled. Her heart felt lighter already.

He offered his usual boyish grin before escorting her inside the ballroom. Many an eye turned in their direction, speculative glances followed them, an older lady on a young man's arm. Her cheeks heated at the image they must present. She hoped no one ever guessed she lusted for the man at her side.

Selwood remained with her when they rejoined her friends, participating in a lively discussion on furnishings that would have bored any other man to tears. The other matrons—pleased to have a young, handsome man join their circle—flirted with him shamelessly. Selwood flattered her friends outrageously in return, casting sidelong glances at her when she laughed at her friends' blushes. She found those little looks and teasing remarks more than a little disconcerting, yet she couldn't find the nerve to join in and tease him too. After a while, Selwood took his leave, wishing them all a pleasant evening.

As he departed, Phoebe followed his retreat. Selwood's dark form cut a wide path through the gaudily dressed gentlemen in attendance. She let her gaze stray lower, admiring the movement of his muscular thighs encased in dark silk. An unwise wish flittered through her mind that it could be him joining her in bed. *Impossible*. She cursed her foolishness under her breath as Lord Selwood departed the ballroom with a spring in his step, no doubt eager to find someone younger to charm.

Once his dark head disappeared from sight, anticipation and anxiety clawed at her belly. Could she really go through with this? Could she really make love to a mystery gentleman this very evening?

The gentlemen about her—some wearing more finery than she—didn't really appeal. Yet she wasn't acquainted with every man here tonight. Selwood must have someone else in mind for her midnight rendezvous and he was on his way to speak to them.

A trilling laugh grated over Phoebe's senses as her stepson entered the ballroom with Lady Jocelyn Clifford hanging on his arm. Wonderful. Warminster could parade his future wife on his arm openly before his friends, yet she couldn't attempt to engage in a clandestine tryst herself without him alerting his oldest friend.

When he became detained in conversation with a somewhat dull-witted acquaintance, Lady Jocelyn approached her, all shy smiles and clinging hands.

"Lady Warminster," she gushed. "You are positively radiant tonight."

"You are too, my dear. Peach brings out the blue of your eyes."

Lady Jocelyn bounced on her toes. "Mamma said it was perfect for this evening, and I do agree with her. Yet I wondered if my blue silk might have pleased Lord Warminster more. Did I make the correct choice? I do think you will have the right of it."

Phoebe recoiled from the girl's simpering. Would her stepson really tie himself to this brainless, indecisive chit?

Luckily, Warminster's approach saved her from further conversation.

"Ah, Lady Warminster," her stepson began, "how are you enjoying the evening?"

"Very well, Warminster. I am amply entertained." She glanced about the ballroom. Despite her irritation with him for inflicting Lady Jocelyn on her daily during the party, and sending his friend to spy on her behavior, she would not cause a scene. She had to play along with his charade of worthless fop until the last guest departed and then he would vanish again on state business. That moment couldn't come soon enough. "The evening has been a delight. You must be proud all your efforts have borne fruit."

"Yes, my party is an unqualified success." Warminster chuckled, glancing down at Lady Jocelyn with a smile. Then he leaned closer. "People shall talk of this house party for many years to come. And not because of some petulant, tawdry affair either."

At the superior glance Warminster cast at her, Phoebe decided she *would* open her bedchamber door to whatever gentleman Selwood sent her tonight. Yet she affected a laugh as if she agreed with her stepson.

"Have you seen Selwood?"

Given that both Warminster and Lady Jocelyn asked the same question at once, Phoebe felt certain she could be forgiven for gaping. She glanced between them and noticed discomfort on both sides. "I'm unsure. He left the ballroom a short time ago."

Warminster smiled at the news.

A frown creased Lady Jocelyn's brow too.

She sidled up to Warminster. "Is he avoiding me?" she whispered.

"Of course he isn't, my dear." He captured her arm. "I'm sure my friend has simply been detained by conversation elsewhere."

Lady Jocelyn glanced about, a hopeful expression lighting her features. Why would she be so keen to become better acquainted with Lord Selwood when she had Warminster hanging on her every word?

Phoebe stood between the pair for some time while they remained silent. Quite discomforted by the lack of conversation, she excused herself, yet she couldn't shake the idea that Lady Jocelyn had designs on Selwood too. She already had Warminster eating from the palm of her dainty hand. If she set her sights on Lord Selwood, they could be at each other's throats.

The two men—now both two and twenty—had been great friends since childhood.

A woman shouldn't come between them.

When Phoebe eventually retired, she was a bundle of nervous energy. She changed for bed, dismissed the maid then turned to extinguish the candles. Her hands shook as she snuffed each flame until she stood in the weak illumination from the fire.

She stared at the glowing embers a long time before picking up her pitcher of water to douse them. If she saw who came to her bed tonight, she feared she'd never go through with the endeavor. Selwood appeared to be correct: she'd be uncomfortable seeing her lover's face. Darkness definitely appealed.

Once the room harbored nothing but shadows, Phoebe stumbled to the bed, slipped from her nightgown, and settled against the carved headboard to wait. After a few minutes, her door creaked open. A spill of light brightened the chamber briefly, and she caught sight of a tall form entering her room. The floorboards groaned as the man came closer, fabric slithered in the dark, and then the foot of the bed dipped.

"Enchantée, ma belle."

A Frenchman? Phoebe wracked her brain for his identity. There had been none on Warminster's list that she could remember. She inched up the bed.

"Do not be afraid, *S'il vous plait.* Your Lord Selwood 'as sent me for your pleasure."

Although surprised Selwood had sent a Frenchman to her bed, the stranger's cultured accent reassured her. Phoebe relaxed and moved her legs from the sitting position she was in toward her midnight guest.

After a brief slither of sound, he captured one foot. "You 'ave such délicat toes. Perfection."

The stranger kissed the tip of her big toe. Then another, and another. When he surrounded her toe with the warmth of his mouth and sucked, Phoebe gasped. No one had ever touched her feet before with such reverence. When he released her toe, he did not stop kissing. He bathed her whole foot in soft kisses. Some—like the ones pressed into the arch with more pressure—made her squirm. When he released her right foot altogether it was so he could turn his attention to her left.

The Frenchman's hot breath rasped over her senses and when he was done he raised her leg. Phoebe gasped as he perched her calf on his hot, bare shoulder. Shocked that her lover might be completely naked already, Phoebe wriggled higher up the bed.

"'Ave you 'ad a change of 'eart, *ma belle?*" Her Frenchman stilled, but his churning breath rang loud in the room.

"No," she whispered. "Not at all. I like this very much."

"*Dieu merci!*"

The fervent exclamation drove a laugh from her lips. She didn't want this French stranger to go, she'd just been surprised that he might be naked. At least her first foray into scandalous pleasure would be expedient.

The flesh now pressed against her leg

shifted as he continued to kiss a path up her inner thigh. "If only I could see you, *ma belle.*"

Given the way he had her arranged, Phoebe was grateful for the blanketing darkness. She couldn't have borne this pose in the light. She couldn't stop her blushing if she tried.

Her Frenchman shifted again, dragging her other leg onto his other shoulder so her feet rested on his back, her knees open wide. A breath of air brushed her curls. Phoebe tensed, anticipation lifting her hips restlessly. The man dragged in a deep, loud breath, and then his lips touched her sensitive inner thigh. That kiss wasn't where she'd expected it to be. She'd expected, hoped, he'd go straight to her nub first, but he took his time, pressing light kisses around her lower lips, teasing but not fulfilling her wish for more.

Phoebe crossed her ankles behind his head and nudged him forward.

Her reward—resistance and a deep laugh. "We 'ave all night, *ma belle.* I want to feast on you the way you deserve. Slowly—" he pressed a kiss low down, next to the entrance to her body—"and with reverence. You deserve nothing less."

Phoebe shuddered, her body rippling with pleasure at the slow loving her Frenchman lavished on her. She was in the hands of a master of seduction. His words set her body aflame. As the urge to beg for him to claim her filled her mouth, she pressed her head harder against the pillow, determined to control her impatience.

As if sensing her capitulation, he slid his warm hand under her bottom and tilted her hips. His hot open-mouthed kiss on her sex dragged a long moan from her lungs and she fisted her hands in the sheets to rein in her need for more.

Warmth flooded her senses, and then the unmistakable brush of a wet tongue. The Frenchman parted her lips with his talented mouth, sliding upward to briefly touch her nub before retreating. She would die. He did it again, repeating that soft touch so often that she growled aloud at the incompleteness she felt. Another chuckle, and then he applied firmer pressure.

To her relief, he moved higher to her nub. At the sensation of suction, Phoebe curled up from the mattress to hold her lover's head firmly in place. The soft, silky hair threaded through her fingers was long enough to grip. She tightened her hold as he ate at her greedily, lapping with his tongue, sucking hard on the nub then biting gently on her lower lips.

The feverish assault on her senses pushed her dangerously close to the edge. She clutched his hair tight, pulling his face harder against her. The edge loomed. She was going to come right now. Any moment. She burst to—

The Frenchman removed his lips, and pushed her knees apart. "*Non*. Do not rush, *mon amour*. We 'ave all night for pleasure."

Phoebe panted. "No!" She'd been so close.

Her lover wriggled from her clutching fingers and turned her to her side, wedging his thigh between hers as he slid in behind. He captured her restless hands. In this position Phoebe couldn't even clench her thighs together to finish what he'd started.

Frustrated by his dominance, by the withheld release just moments away, she ground her backside into his lap. The hard ridge of his erection burned her skin, and a warning growl rumbled behind her.

"I never would 'ave imagined you so impatient."

His lips caressed the apple of her shoulder, his hands smoothed over her thigh as Phoebe struggled to get her breathing under control. She glanced over her shoulder but, given how dark she'd made her own chamber, she couldn't discern who held her. "Bossy Frenchman."

His lips pressed to her turned cheek and then another growl rumbled through her lover. The Frenchman dragged Phoebe to her hands and knees then moved in close behind. Something heavy, hot and eager settled into the crease of her bottom. She eagerly widened her stance and tilted her hips to better receive him.

But as before, her lover wouldn't rush. Her hips were grasped gently, thumbs kneading her lower back in slow circles, as he rubbed his erection into the crease. Blast it all, this man would torture her forever. She needed more than torture. She needed release. Phoebe shifted her weight to one hand and moved the other between her legs to build her desire once more.

He caught on quickly and covered her moving fingers with his own. The dual attention excited her unbearably and she moaned as her lover nudged into her body and then thrust deep.

"*Merci! Tu es magnifique!*" he whispered against her shoulder.

While she adjusted to his surprising girth, his fingers slipped and slid with hers, working to build her passion higher. When he thrust, then pulled out completely before sinking deep into her body, Phoebe moaned.

Sensations built swiftly while her lover used all his skill to coax her legs wider, to help her accept more of him. His thick length invaded her body, battering her senses into submission. She moaned at the joy of surrender.

A heavy rising tension gripped her as his sure hard thrusts claimed her completely. She opened to him, letting him use her as he saw fit.

Behind her, the Frenchman grunted, a hand clutched her hip tight. "Together we will come, *mon amour*," he whispered. "Are you ready?"

"Yes, oh God, yes."

Phoebe rubbed harder against her nub while behind her, the Frenchman thrust deep then ground their hips together in a tight circle. Her body clenched and then shook violently, dragging a loud wail from her lungs at the intensity.

He shuddered, and then thrust hard three times as he pumped his seed into her body. His heavy weight fell over her, cocooning her in blistering heat. Phoebe hung her head as she struggled for breath. Never. Not once had her husband affected her senses like this. What she'd thought she wanted, and what she'd gotten, surpassed her every desire.

She'd have to remember to thank Lord Selwood the next time she saw him. But that could wait till morning. She would have this Frenchman again if she could.

CHAPTER THREE

JONATHAN SIPPED his coffee behind the day's newssheet while the houseguests clattered and chattered over breakfast. He supposed he was being rude by not conversing with them, but he needed the dry analytical content of the paper to control his raging arousal.

Lady Jocelyn sat across from him, daintily eating her breakfast and sipping her tea. But she had stretched out her leg and was currently running her toe up and down his trouser in a brazen flirtation.

However, what aroused Jonathan was Lady Warminster's presence across the room, fixing herself a heaped plate of food. He could usually bear the sight of her without an outward reaction, but today her smile tortured him. She looked smugly happy, content and, given the way her lips lifted for no obvious reason, he wondered if she was thinking of last night.

Jonathan tucked his legs under his chair, turned the page, and tried to concentrate on the goings on in parliament he'd missed during the recent sessions, but the paper couldn't hold his interest. He lowered a corner as Lady Warminster sank into a chair at his side.

"Lord Selwood, I didn't expect to see you so early in the day." She reached for her silver.

He hadn't actually slept because of her. He folded the paper and set it in his lap, waving away the footman eager to take it from him. He might just need it to escape the room without drawing undue attention to the condition he was in. "Good morning, my lady."

The blonde beauty smiled, lips lifting enough to torture. Jonathan glanced away. Was she thinking of last night and her mysterious French lover?

Across the table, Lady Jocelyn winked at him.

He turned back to Lady Warminster as she cleared her throat.

"I must thank you, Selwood, for your advice last evening. I believe I've never had a better night's rest."

Jonathan coughed. She hadn't had a wink of sleep 'till the early hours of the morning. He'd made damn sure of that in his guise as her French lover. "I'm glad."

Still, the memory of his deception, imitating his late mother's people, sat ill with him. But if the lady had known she'd entertained him—a gentleman younger than her stepson—in her bed he'd have been kicked from the room posthaste. However, the French had a way with words that never ceased to arouse his lovers. So he'd disguised his voice and used the cover of the darkened chamber to share the night with the lovely Lady Warminster. He couldn't regret that fact.

"Morning Selwood," Lizzy sang out as she swept into the room. "What are you doing here so early?"

Thank heavens for small mercies. The presence of his sister would surely dampen any amorous inclinations. "And a good morning to you too, Lizzy. I am eating as you can clearly see."

Lizzy filled her plate to alarming proportions, avoided eye contact with the lingering bachelors, and sank into the chair on his other side. Jonathan eyed the plate. "If you consume all that you shall have the gentlemen stampeding in the other direction. Be sure not to overdo," he whispered.

Lizzy's lips lifted in a sweet smile. "*Occupe-toi de tes affaires*, Selwood."

"*Sois sage, enfant.*" The warning quip to behave rolled off his tongue in French so swiftly that he didn't consider the wisdom of what he was saying and how. Silver clattered against china to his right, and dread trickled through him. He turned to Lady Warminster. She stared at her plate with fixed attention, grasping her retrieved knife and fork with a tight grip, an alarmingly high color pinked her cheeks.

Concerned, he set his fingertips to her hand. "Are you at all well, my lady?"

The countess shrugged and his fingers were dislodged. "Yes, yes, everything is fine." Then she hastily shoved food into her mouth. Unsure if he had given himself away or not, Jonathan finished his coffee. Given that his sister's presence had a strong cooling effect on his desires, he no longer had any need to linger at the table. He excused himself and, despite failing in his mission to speak privately to Lady Jocelyn, he went off to find his friend.

As usual, Lord Warminster was in his study, resplendent in shockingly bright shades of green silk. Warminster glanced up swiftly as the sound of the door opening reached him then buried his head in his confidential report again.

Jonathan paced the room until he was done. "I came to say goodbye."

"Forget it." Warminster advised in his usual voice, devoid of the grating cheeriness. "You are here for the duration."

Jonathan stared at his friend, or soon to be ex-friend if he ever learned where he had spent last night. He couldn't stay. He couldn't be trusted not to expose himself to Warminster's stepmother in more ways than one. "I do have other responsibilities, old man."

Warminster crossed his arms over his chest, and Jonathan noticed he sported yet another garishly vulgar gold fob chain. He really did dress the part of a fool well but he'd never make the mistake of believing the lie.

"Elizabeth is here too. She's your responsibility. You couldn't hope to have a better excuse to linger around the ladies."

"Ha." Jonathan shook his head. Lizzy refused to follow his advice, and after many a pitched battle, he'd given up. Besides, life had become infinitely more peaceful since he stopped trying to force her down the matrimonial path. Once Lizzy ceased all her blustering, he found her surprisingly good company. However, most men did not consider their sisters' happiness when planning such alliances. Like Warminster they remained at loggerheads for all eternity, determined to marry them off for political and financial gain. "Lizzy will go her own way regardless of my presence."

"She needs a leash."

Jonathan wearily sank into a chair as the exertions of last night, the lack of sleep, overwhelmed him. He planned to put his feet up and take a nice long nap when he returned home to Dalemain Court. "Then someone else will have to fit it to her. She bites."

Staying for the whole of the house party might provide him with the opportunity to woo Lady Jocelyn out from under Warminster's nose, yet after the adventure of last night the debutante's charms were less appealing than they previously were.

Warminster looked up, a scowl creasing his face into fury. "Do you not care how she is perceived by others? The gossip about her is quite offensive. I considered calling Perkins out last night over some unflattering comments about her ability to make a match. I simply cannot lose my temper around these fools."

Amused by his friend's strong reaction, Jonathan leaned forward. "Settle your feathers. Have you not worked it out yet? She has a grand plan in mind for her life. Marriage does not feature in it at all."

"Ridiculous. You've let her run wild."

"Well, if you believe that's the case, my friend, you're welcome to attempt to take her in hand," Jonathan urged with a teasing smile. "Just don't come complain to me later when the wound turns septic."

Warminster's skin darkened, his lips pressed tight together. The other man didn't remain silent long. "If this is how you speak of Elizabeth then it is not surprising she remains unmarried."

"Oh, for God sake." He was too weary for Warminster's games. "You know Lizzy very well. She won't marry without love. Our parents' unhappy union taught us too well. And don't pretend this is all my doing that she's still here to tempt you. If you're so concerned, you should have trusted that she could keep your confidences. You should have wed her years ago and been done with these foolish games that you don't care about her."

"Don't be ridiculous." Warminster scowled, tugging on his pea green waistcoat. "In my line of work a man can't have an intelligent female clinging permanently to his arm. She could be badly hurt if anyone believed she was in my confidence."

Secretly, Jonathan pitied Warminster. Perhaps his friend didn't understand his sister after all. "You'd be surprised how well Lizzy can defend herself. Just last week she blackened Lord Archer's eye for touching her arm."

Warminster's eyes widened. "She didn't?"

"Knocked him right on his presumptuous arse. I haven't laughed so hard in ages." He shrugged. "At least, not since the last swain came to pester her."

Warminster stood suddenly and started pacing. After three turns around the room, he stopped at the door to the terrace. "Just how well can Elizabeth defend herself?"

"I've not trained her, if that's what you're asking, but she does have a suitably robust temper and tends to use whatever is at hand."

His friend pivoted, eyebrows raised high. "Like poor, potted plants?"

Jonathan laughed weakly. "Oh, hell. Has Lizzy gotten physical with one of your guests? I bet Mr. Perkins regrets following her onto the terrace now."

"Not Perkins." Warminster ran both hands through his pale hair, disturbing the precise curls.

Alarmed, Jonathan sat forward. "Warminster? Are you all right?"

The other man nodded, but then shook his head. "A man, a stranger, was found just outside that terrace door this morning. Trussed like a bird with the shattered remnants of a potted petunia at his feet. I had wondered who'd dealt with him."

"A friend of yours or another in the profession?"

Warminster nodded and his face paled horribly. "The latter."

"Well, Lizzy appears no worse for wear this morning," Jonathan mused. "In fact, I thought her downright cheerful."

"Good. Good." Warminster however appeared anything but. "I need to speak with her."

Now that would be an interesting conversation, certainly one not to miss. *So much for Lizzy's good mood.* He wearily dragged himself to his feet. "They were at breakfast when I left them."

"They?"

"Lizzy and your mother."

"Stepmother," Warminster corrected as he dragged Jonathan from the room. But the ladies were no longer at the table. They stood some distance away in the garden.

Warminster hailed them cheerfully and swiftly dragged Jonathan's sister aside for a private tête-à-tête. Jonathan watched them for a long moment and, seeing Lizzy didn't appear likely to kneecap his friend immediately, he let his gaze shift to the countess.

Lady Warminster appeared to be looking

everywhere but at him. Disappointed, he glanced at his sister and his friend where they stood in deep conversation. No sign of trouble yet. "Would you care to sit, my lady?"

Her back stiffened. "No, thank you."

He shrugged off the rebuff. If she had worked out who had shared her bed last night, and didn't like it, then that was her problem. He distinctly remembered the lady singing his praises repeatedly during the night. She might fool herself today that she'd been imposed upon, but Jonathan remembered that she'd enjoyed his attentions thoroughly.

He sat with a groan, and swiveled so he could lie upon the bench, pressing one arm across his eyes. He'd rest here a few moments then return home.

Phoebe discreetly watched Lord Selwood fall asleep on the hard, stone bench while she tried to control her pounding heart, but her pulse raced with the fear that she had not just been indiscreet, she'd been monumentally stupid. How could she have taken a man to her bed and not tried harder to determine his identity.

To be sure, the French accent had distracted her. She'd forgotten Selwood's late mother was a French émigré, but the quick snippet of conversation she'd heard between Selwood and his sister at breakfast had brought the memory flooding back. Selwood spoke French fluently enough for her to suspect that Warminster might enlist his help in his highly secretive work. But had she really taken a man to her bed whose age was so much lower than hers?

Why would he desire an older woman?

She faced him fully. The longish, dark hair fanned out over the stone bench was of similar length to her lover's. The expertly tailored jacket and waistcoat hid a broad and possibly muscled chest. Phoebe let her gaze travel along the strong legs, large feet and—when her gaze rose again—the obvious outline of an erection tenting his dark trousers.

"May I help you, my lady?" Selwood watched her, a wicked smile lingering on his lips.

Appalled to be caught staring, Phoebe spun about. No! She simply could not have made love to him. But when she heard Selwood climb to his feet and move to stand behind her, she trembled.

"I forgot. You like the cloak of darkness to hide your desires behind. Did you enjoy your view, *ma belle*?"

Phoebe raised a hand to her throat. "Don't speak like that."

A light touch ghosted over her back. "Why not? You didn't object last night. In fact, you were quite vocal in your appreciation of certain conversations. I particularly enjoyed the one about your breasts."

She pressed her hands to her flaming cheeks. "Please. Stop."

"That wasn't what you said last night."

Phoebe swung around. "How dare you?"

A pleased grin spread across Selwood's handsome face. "Why not me? I met all of your criteria. Clean, experienced, available, and discreet. No one could possibly suspect I was in your bed last night. And I would do it again to 'ear you scream in pleasure, *mon amour*."

Phoebe's heart beat frantically as Selwood added the French accent to his last words. "Warminster will kill you when he finds out. You know what he is. Were you tired of his friendship?"

Selwood's arrogant smile chilled her. "No, not tired of it, but things change. He set me to watch you last evening and his desire happened to coincide with mine. Can you imagine he placed me in the bedchamber beside yours with orders to beat any man to a pulp if they so much as looked at you twice? It wasn't hard to convince me, but I put on a good show of resistance just the same."

She stared up into his dark eyes and her body quivered, utterly out of control.

"I would make love to you in the light, *ma belle*. Bring you such pleasure that you would scream my name for all to hear. I could rest your back against that broad oak tree, fall to my knees at your feet and delve beneath your skirts. Would you like to watch me lick your nub until desire overtakes you?"

Phoebe shook her head to banish the erotic image. This surely must be a dream.

"Or would you like me to lure you to the center of the maze, push you to your knees and take you from behind again? When we were joined, I could feel every intimate shudder of your body, every gasp from your lips, and hear every plea for me to fuck you harder."

Selwood slid his fingers along her arm, drawing heat from every pore of her skin. To her horror, she could feel moisture flooding from between her legs. Phoebe pressed her thighs together as he moved closer.

"Look at me."

Hesitantly, she glanced up. Lord Selwood's dark gaze burned into her composure. Her breasts grew heavy, nipples hardening to painful peaks under her thin day gown. Selwood's gaze swept across her chest—lingering on her breasts in a most unsettling way. His smile widened. "No corset."

Phoebe dragged in a breath as he moved his hands toward her. He didn't touch. He was only teasing her with the idea of it. Yet her body believed what it wanted to. She burned for more.

"In case you miss me, *ma belle*, I'm not adverse to a daytime rendezvous. I am under Warminster's orders to stay for the entire house party, so I'll be in my bedchamber, and at your disposal, for the whole afternoon."

Her mind whirled. Selwood was staying in the house, in the bedchamber next to hers for the whole week of this godforsaken house party. She'd have to lock the doors to keep him out. To keep herself in her own room too.

"Now, as much as I'd like to continue our stirring discussion, you must excuse me. The conversation between your son and my sister looks to be reaching a critical point. Warminster might do better with his head on his shoulders. Lizzy appears incensed. *Au revoir*."

While Phoebe blinked away the effects of Selwood's verbal seduction, he strode off, collected his furious sister, and disappeared around the ornamental pond.

Good God. I'm doomed.

With just a few short words, Selwood had

reduced her to a mass of quivering need. She couldn't get the images he'd planted in her mind to go away. The idea of the young, muscled man pleasuring her in the garden brought greater yearning coursing through her. She wanted him. She wanted to come again against that talented mouth, on the thick cock she'd surrendered to last night. Damn it, she wanted everything.

Warminster stalked past her on his way to the house. "Bloody confounding creature," he muttered. "I doubt I shall ever understand those Olivers."

Silently, Phoebe agreed with him.

CHAPTER FOUR

JONATHAN STRETCHED on the wide bed with a deep, satisfied groan. That sleep was just what he'd needed to face the house party activities of the evening, and an evening spent in the delectable countess' company. He tucked his hands behind his head and grinned. Phoebe was every bit as passionate as he'd suspected. Even more so. He craved her soft body again already.

His cock swelled at the memory of last night's adventure. He rolled from the bed and headed for the washbasin. The jug of cool water should dampen his desire for now. He scrubbed and washed with brutal efficiency, dousing any lingering lust.

Voices outside caught his attention. He snatched up a towel and moved to stand by the window, hiding his naked state behind the heavy velvet drapes. From his vantage point two floors up, Jonathan spied his sister and Lord Warminster deep within the maze. Lizzy appeared angry again, if her clenched fists were any indication.

Warminster took a pace toward her and then he disappeared from view. Jonathan stretched up on his toes to see what'd happened. Warminster staggered up from the ground as Lizzy swept 'round the corner of the maze.

He shouldn't laugh at his friend, but for a spy, he was damned unprepared for an attack. Lizzy must have used her favorite trick and swept his feet out from under him. Poor bastard. He'd be livid if she'd sullied his pristine attire.

Since his sister didn't require his assistance yet, Jonathan turned back to the room. To his delight Lady Warminster stood at the connecting doorway, one hand on the knob, mouth hanging open.

She stared, swallowed but didn't say a word.

Despite Jonathan's intention to remain cool-headed around the woman, his cock filled. The countess licked her lips. "Ah, Lady Warminster, Phoebe, did you require me?"

Her gaze remained fixed at his groin. Trying to hide a pleased smile, Jonathan strolled toward her, circled behind, and then pushed the connecting door shut. Just to be sure they remained uninterrupted he turned the key in the lock too.

He re-crossed the room at the same lazy pace and sank into a low armless chair. For good measure, he widened his stance, displaying himself.

Phoebe's cheeks pinked. She gulped and then dragged her gaze up to his face. "Put something on."

Instead of complying, Jonathan ran a hand across his bare chest, over his abdomen, and clasped his cock in a loose grip. "I'll put *you* on if you like. Come over here, *ma belle*. Let's see if you still fit me."

Phoebe shook her head then slowly closed the distance between them. For the moment, he didn't mind that her gaze remained on his throbbing cock. He didn't mind that she saw him only as a means of receiving pleasure. He wanted her to see him as a desirable man, not the awkward youth he'd been. They were already friends. Everything else was a delicious bonus as far as he was concerned.

Jonathan leaned forward to capture her blue muslin gown with both hands and tugged her closer. When their gazes connected, Phoebe's eyes widened. "What am I doing? I shouldn't be here."

He didn't answer her. He didn't want to frighten her off by discussing the rightness or wrongness of their liaison now. So he tugged again until she fell into his lap, and buried his face in her delicious white skin. He kissed and nipped at the column of her throat hungrily, keen to distract her with desire.

Phoebe's hands fluttered over his skin then she held on tight. He cast a quick glance at her face. She'd closed her eyes against the image of what they were doing. Jonathan didn't care for that, but for now he'd let her have her way. He stretched to find the bottom of her skirts and swiftly captured her restless stocking-clad leg, massaging her knee, curling his fingers into her soft flesh.

At her gasp of pleasure, he shifted her on his lap so she sat astride him.

Wide, pale green eyes stared at him then snapped shut again on a whimper.

With both hands now under her bunched up skirts, Jonathan had unfettered access. He smoothed his hands over her skin in gentle sweeps, and then dug his fingertips into her bottom to move her closer to his erection. At the contact, Phoebe squirmed.

He buried his face in her neck again to hide his smile. She could easily become addicted to the pleasure he gave. But it might take some doing for her to accept the gap in their ages hardly mattered. He could be patient when he wanted something badly enough. And he wanted to make love to her again so very badly.

With his teeth, he tugged her gown off one shoulder and then shifted the bodice low. One delightful pert breast popped free and he eagerly took the hard peak into his mouth. Jonathan tongued her and nipped her delicate skin while he rocked her hips against the hard ridge of his erection.

Phoebe whimpered impatiently, digging her fingers into his hair to hold his head tight to her breast. Her hips shifted again, rising up as if attempting to mount him. To help, Jonathan released his hold and grasped his cock, lifting the stiff length away from his belly. Phoebe rose higher and sat on the tip.

Jonathan released her breast as she impaled herself.

She squirmed a little, inching him inside hesitantly. He held still, forced his shaft upright while she slowly accepted him. With a cock as thick as his it didn't pay to rush his entry. He'd hate to cause her pain. When her wet lower lips touched his fist he withdrew his hand and played with her clitoris. His lover gasped then bit her lip as she descended another delicious inch.

When he was fully encased, stuffed as high into her body as he could get, Jonathan clasped her hips and moved her along his length. Phoebe let out a low moan and clutched his shoulders. When he slid her down him she moaned again.

"You see, Phoebe, we are an exceptionally good fit. What a delightfully welcoming hostess. Ah," he gasped as pleasure built.

Jonathan lowered his mouth to her breast again, tugging the pert nipple into his mouth and sucked hard. Phoebe moved on his length, setting her own rhythm to their coupling, pushing him always deeper inside. She clutched his nape, holding his hair tight in her grip, never letting him release her breast for long.

The lady hummed as they fucked, proving to him she was enjoying his skills immensely. Jonathan touched her nub again, strumming lightly over the hard peak. Phoebe shuddered, breaking her rhythm and settling low upon him. She left him deep but moved her hips in slow rotations, grinding him deeper than before.

Jonathan released her breast to watch her. Her eyes were closed, lip caught between even white teeth, a look of intense concentration on her face. He cupped her skull and her eyes flew open, staring at him with a passion-bright gaze.

"You have me so deep, my darling, so deep and high into your body that we are fused into one. I'm going to enjoy every delicious shudder as you peak on my cock. That's it, one more brush, one more moment. That's it—" her eyes widened—"that's it, come on me, darling."

The countess' breath caught, and then she shuddered, clenching him in a tight vise of warmth. Jonathan gritted his teeth at the sensations, letting her focus on the pleasure that continued to wrack her body, letting her become aware he had watched it all. Her head landed on his shoulder and she drew in deep, desperate gasps of air.

He cradled her close, loving the weight of her in his arms, on his cock. Breathing her desire. Had she realized they had never kissed? Not once had their lips even come close to one another. But he wanted that now. He wanted to taste the countess' contentment and have her recognize him as the cause.

He nuzzled her neck, kissed a path across her cheek, and captured her soft lips. Phoebe appeared startled, yet she closed her eyes and let him take what he needed. She parted her lips and he swept his tongue inside. She tasted delightful, like warm caramel and he couldn't help but continue his assault. Her small hands closed about his head, gentling him when he would have plundered. He was still firm, still achingly hard within her when she started to move.

With his lover's active participation, he thrust within her tight confines. It wasn't enough, he needed to move, to bury himself deep again and again. He craved friction.

Jonathan stood, lifting Phoebe with him while they kissed and stumbled toward his bed. He lowered her down to the soft, rumpled sheets but kept their lips connected.

The countess had a wicked tongue and she used it to inflame him. She invaded his mouth to match the lazy pace of his thrusts and he closed his eyes at the powerful need that rose up in him. He wanted to thrust hard, take control of this woman, and possess her in every way possible.

He shifted and looked down on her. Wide, pale green eyes regarded him, a lingering smile tugged at her lips. He reached for her hips and dragged her to the end of the bed. Phoebe glanced down.

He took himself in hand, rubbing his wet cockhead across her nub. She panted hard from the sensation and he reinserted himself in a slow thrust. Her spine arched as he reached her limit and he grasped her breast tight.

With one hand on her hip, one squeezing her breast, he set a furious pace, thrusting hard into her body. Phoebe fluttered her fingers over her bunched up skirts and then slipped them low to her nub. She touched herself while their gazes held, pushing his desire high at the erotic sight. Jonathan rolled her nipple between his thumb and fingers, pinching and drawing on the peak.

She teased herself frantically. She curled up to watch him pound into her. Her curiosity was his undoing. Jonathan's release tightened his balls, unstoppable desire swept over him as he came so hard he shouted out. While his body shuddered, his lover cried out her release too, and then she collapsed to the soft bedding, as sated as he. Jonathan followed, keeping his cock buried deep but rolling until Phoebe lay boneless over his chest.

He held her tight, dragged in the desire-scented air around them, and wished they didn't ever have to leave this room. Phoebe seemed content to lie with him. He let his hands travel over her gown covered back and wished he'd taken the time to undress her. Maybe next time—tonight if he was a very lucky man—he might have her bare between his sheets.

But this time there would be no darkness to hide behind. He wanted to see where he kissed, where he touched, and to watch her face every time she reached for bliss.

"Dinner will be announced soon. I have to go." She squirmed, expelled him from her body, and slid off his chest without meeting his gaze. He captured her hand to hold her to the bed.

"Wait." Jonathan surged up and captured her lips in a possessive kiss. He couldn't let her get away with that look of embarrassment on her face. Their lust was natural, addictive, and he wanted her to accept it now before anyone or anything else intruded.

Phoebe crawled into his lap, deepening their kiss until they were both panting.

When they parted, Jonathan held her snug in his arms and simply looked at her. She was beautiful, breathtaking, and all his, if he got his way.

After a little while, she relaxed and her lips curled into an exasperated smile. "Why in heavens name would you wish to make love to me?"

That was an easy question to answer. "Because." He grabbed her hand and wedged it between them. She wrapped her fingers around his growing length, and then to his delight—tightened. "You've had an enlarging affect on me for some time. I'd rather explore what might be between us than ignore it another day."

CHAPTER FIVE

"THERE SHOULDN'T BE anything between us. Are you mad?" Phoebe escaped Selwood's hands before he could distract her again with kisses.

The younger man followed, striding proudly across the room in absolutely nothing at all. "Not in the least."

The earl ran a hand through his dark hair and the effect on her senses as his muscles flexed was frightening. She wanted nothing more than to curl up against that broad chest and seek the pleasure he so readily gave. Phoebe pressed the heel of her hand to her brow to expel the image of his body. "This is insane. I shouldn't share your bed. This cannot happen again."

He shrugged. "You're a grown woman.

You're not cuckolding a husband. Who's to say aught about the matter?"

"Warminster," she reminded him. Really did the man have no sense? The last man to cross her stepson had found himself impressed on one of the king's ships and bound for the colonies.

Selwood set his feet wide, hands resting on his hips. "Warminster can bluster all he likes, but he won't stand in my way. Besides, he owes me."

"Owes you?" Her voice rose to a shrill pitch but she couldn't control it. "Am I some sort of reward then?"

His dark gaze pierced her. "Don't be ridiculous, woman. That's not what I meant at all."

Phoebe shook her head. "This is impossible. I'll not be responsible for ending your friendship."

Selwood approached and despite her good intentions, she allowed him to draw her tight against his chest. His skin was warm against her cheek and she breathed in the heady scent of him. Without meaning to, she curled her arms about his bare waist and clutched him tight. His erection, already firm again, prodded her belly.

"Warminster will become used to the idea in due time," he murmured, skimming his hands down her spine. "He's not completely unreasonable."

"Do you have any idea of how many weapons he has in this house?" Phoebe pressed her lips to Selwood's chest, imagining the horror of that number.

"I imagine as many as I." Selwood pressed a kiss to her hair. "Have some faith in my powers of persuasion."

"Oh, I'm well acquainted with your powers." She pushed out of his arms. "That's what's landed me in trouble in the first place."

He smiled but said nothing more.

"I have to go." But her hands wanted nothing more than to stay and explore all that divine muscle.

"Yes, dinner will be announced soon. You have Warminster's guests to entertain."

Phoebe wrinkled her nose. "Please don't remind me. I will be relieved when this week is over and we get Moreton Hall to ourselves again."

"I'll see you at dinner then." Selwood bowed extravagantly.

Disconcerted to have a naked man bow so elegantly to her, she rushed from the room to get ready for the evening.

While she bathed and dressed, Phoebe considered what Lord Selwood had said. He intended for her stepson to learn of their liaison, that they were lovers. Warminster would not be happy about that. He would make her life even more difficult.

Phoebe entered the drawing room with considerable trepidation to mingle with Warminster's guests. Although by rights she should have acted as his hostess, his prickly disposition made it impossible to do so. So far, the most he'd allowed was letting her order the tea to be served in the drawing room.

"I see Lord Selwood has joined our party," Lady Clifford purred loudly in her ear. "Such a handsome, virile man. What we wouldn't give to be ten years younger, eh?"

She gasped. Given that Lady Clifford's age was greater than her own, she couldn't possibly hope to appeal to a younger man. Mind you, Phoebe thought that of herself less than twenty-four hours ago. "Yes, I suppose so." When she glanced across the room she spotted Lord Selwood chatting with Warminster. The odd pairing—one draped in claret silk, the other clothed in blue superfine —seemed as cozy as usual. That would end.

Lady Clifford tapped her arm. "I'm certain he's headed for marriage. See there—" the lady pointed across the room—"he's already got a likely candidate lined up for a wife. A pity for him my daughter favors Lord Warminster at the present moment. But still, Selwood won't have trouble finding an experienced playmate to ease his disappointment. He's still sensible enough to cast his eye about for a willing bed partner while he bides his time. Young men are insatiable."

Aghast at the conversation, Phoebe fanned herself. Of course Selwood would marry, and possibly soon, but could he be after the insipid Lady Jocelyn too? She looked up in time to see Lady Jocelyn insinuate herself in the men's conversation. There was no mistaking the calf's eyes she made as Lord Selwood's gaze fell on her. "I don't know what you mean."

But she did.

Lady Jocelyn had her sights set on both Warminster and Selwood. They were evenly matched in both title and fortune, and the chit could have them at each other's throats before the house party was over. What a mess.

"I've always considered him a crafty one, but there's no point pretending. There'll be an agreement reached before the house party ends." Lady Clifford glanced around, smiling in anticipation.

Phoebe's stomach churned at the image of Selwood in bed with Lady Jocelyn. She wouldn't glance in that direction again.

"Oh, thank heavens. Excuse us, Lady Clifford." Lizzy Oliver clutched her arm and dragged Phoebe toward a blessedly empty corner. "I feared you'd never arrive. Where have you been all afternoon?"

Coming apart at your brother's command. She couldn't very well say that out loud. "Oh, I had a, um, headache," Phoebe improvised.

"Oh, you poor dear. Then a lie down was just the right tonic. You are positively radiant this evening."

"Thank you," she stammered. Lord Selwood—a tonic to restore a woman's vitality? How about the very thing to destroy a lady's peace? Just a glimpse of him set her pulse racing. She wasn't sure how she'd get through the evening knowing he'd be under Lady Jocelyn's thumb soon.

"So, what am I to do about Warminster?"

Phoebe blinked. "What about Warminster?"

"Oh, bother. Can the blathering fool not go away?"

Phoebe turned and spotted Warminster and Selwood making their way toward their quiet corner. Lord Selwood drew closer, handsome in his dark evening coat, and her pulse beat as loud as any parade ground drum. At sixteen, Selwood hadn't seemed comfortable around her.

Their friendship had taken time to develop. Now that they were lovers, Phoebe was the one to be discomforted by him.

Lord Selwood reached them first. "Ladies, why are you both hiding in the corner?" Phoebe searched his face, looking for some hint of what he was thinking, but couldn't detect one flicker of emotion that might give away his feelings.

"Attempting a private conversation," Lizzy hissed. "Go smile at Lady Jocelyn, Selwood. She is eager to capture your attention."

Selwood shuddered. "Perhaps later. I'm more than pleased with my present location."

Although Phoebe tried to hide her relief, Selwood must have noticed her sudden relaxation at his comment. His brow quirked upwards, questioning her reaction without words. She offered a brief smile.

"Ah, Miss Elizabeth." Warminster held out his arm. "Shall we go in to dine?"

Lizzy took in the man's attire and blinked her eyes rapidly.

Phoebe sighed softly. If only Warminster would visit Selwood's tailor and forgo claret satin in his evening attire people would not be so startled when they saw him. It hurt Phoebe's eyes to look at her stepson too closely.

Selwood nudged his sister. "Don't make a scene, Lizzy. People are looking this way."

Reluctantly, Lizzy placed her arm on Warminster's and allowed him to escort her toward the dining room. The resolve on Warminster's face puzzled Phoebe. "What was all that about?"

"Complications." Selwood shrugged. "Shall we go in?"

She expected Selwood to claim her arm but instead, he simply strolled into the dining room at her side, held out a chair for her, and then settled in his. Throughout the meal, he kept the conversation light and entertaining. It was as if what had occurred between them had happened only in her imagination.

Yet, she didn't imagine the way her body ached from his possession, or the tightening of her inner muscles at the memory of his skilled seduction. By the end of the meal, she couldn't decide if she wanted him closer or wanted him to go away to stop the ache.

And she grew tired of the come hither looks Lady Jocelyn kept sending him. Really, must the chit be so obvious?

When Warminster signaled, Phoebe rose with the ladies, leaving the men to their port and cigars. As soon as they reached the hall, Lizzy pulled her away from the others before they reached the drawing room. "I need to talk to you. Now."

At Warminster's study door, Lizzy lifted a hand to her hair, dragged out a pin, and inserted it into the lock. The door swung open silent.

She gaped. "Wherever did you learn to do that?"

"Oh, somewhere." Lizzy tossed her hand negligently. "It comes in handy at times." She pushed her inside the chamber and locked the door behind them, planting her back against the wood. "I need your help."

"My help?" Phoebe squinted into the dark room to check that they were truly alone.

"I need to know how you do it."

Puzzled, she turned. "Do what?"

"Keep the gentlemen at bay, of course. You've been a widow for four years now and not one man has dared attempt to seduce you that I've heard. I must have your secret."

Phoebe choked on a laugh. "My secret is, no one has tried."

"Really? Not one man?"

She nodded hurriedly as she realized she was lying. One man had tried and succeeded admirably. Lord Selwood had only to look at her, smile at her in that knowing way of his, to turn her resolve to mush. But she wouldn't tell his sister any of that. She didn't want to lose her regard.

"Botheration." Lizzy leaned against the

door. "Well, there's nothing left to do except return home. I'm sorry to desert you, but the situation I find myself in is simply impossible."

Concerned, Phoebe moved forward and placed her hand on the younger woman's arm. "Lizzy, what is going on?"

"That mincing fop, Warminster, is trying his hand at matchmaking. He seems to think he can do a better job of it than my brother and spent the whole meal promoting a match between me and that ridiculous Lord Parker."

"Parker? He's still attached to his mother." Phoebe shuddered. "Has Selwood been trying to marry you off too? Hadn't he given up some time ago?"

"Yes, my brother has, but it appears Warminster has a bee in his bonnet and believes every woman should be shackled in matrimony. I'd listen to his advice if he'd consider the matter himself. As it is, he's hardly an admirer of the state. What would he know about the benefits of marriage? No intelligent woman would take him on."

"My thoughts too." Phoebe rubbed her arms. "Listen, you are my invited guest, not Warminster's. I'll do my best to protect you from his plans."

"Would you?" Lizzy launched herself into

her arms and wept, "Why couldn't you have been my sister?"

Phoebe rocked the young woman with a feeling of extreme sadness. She had never felt as welcome with her husband's children as Lizzy had always made her. Warminster barely tolerated her company, and had removed his three younger siblings from her influence as soon as he'd gained the title. Of course, Phoebe would miss them if they'd been the least bit friendly, but chasing after them would have filled the emptiness of her days.

Yet, Lizzy Oliver came to her for advice, for sympathy, and a shoulder to cry on when she needed it. And all of that would end when the girl worked out just how foolish she had been.

Someone scratched on the door. Lizzy jumped, then she squared her shoulders, before offering Phoebe a wan smile. "Thank you."

"Always."

Lizzy opened the door and peeked out. "Oh, it's only you. Thank heavens."

"What's going on in there, Lizzy?" Lord Selwood's voice rumbled over Phoebe's senses, setting her body to humming with anticipation.

When Lizzy glanced at her uncertainly, Phoebe smoothly stepped between them. "Just chatter between women, Selwood."

Although he raised an eyebrow, he appeared to accept her word and didn't question his sister further.

"Well, good night, Phoebe." After pressing a quick kiss to her cheek, Lizzy hurried away, turning up the stairs toward her bedchamber, and leaving her alone with her lover.

"I'd wondered where you'd both gotten to. Shall we rejoin the party?"

Phoebe hesitated. As much as she should rejoin the party, she didn't want to. With no real role to play, and Lizzy headed for her bed, the stupidity of the guests already grated on her nerves. "I believe I will retire."

Selwood nodded. "Well then, goodnight, my lady. Pleasant dreams."

The earl offered her a lopsided smile then sauntered off toward the drawing room. Her heart gave an odd little hitch as he disappeared from view. The ladies in the drawing room would be extremely happy to see him return. She didn't want to imagine how Lady Jocelyn would react.

Phoebe shook her head at the jealousy curling through her belly. She didn't own Selwood. Not at all. He could make love to whomever he liked and probably would. She dragged herself up the long flight of stairs and down the hall to her bedchamber. While her maid undressed her and put away her jewels, she tried not to picture Lady Jocelyn batting her eyelashes or tempting the insatiable Lord Selwood with her young body.

But it was no use. Even as she threw herself into bed, thumping the pillow for good measure, she wondered and worried about where he'd spend the night.

CHAPTER SIX

HOW LONG MUST he remain here in this chattering drawing room before he could escape to Lady Warminster's arms?

By now his lover should be dressed for bed —or undressed if Jonathan was very lucky—and alone in her bedchamber. What kind of reception would he receive tonight? Despite the fact that Phoebe's nipples were noticeably hard beneath her gown during the interminable meal, Jonathan had remained on his best behavior. Keeping his hands down, and away from the delectable orbs displayed so enticingly to his gaze, had taken considerable concentration on his part. He'd probably made mind numbingly boring conversation during the whole of the meal. But he meant to prove his worth outside the bedchamber too.

Finding Phoebe alone with his sister, however, had dimmed his lust. Lizzy's discomfort had turned his thoughts to wonder what Warminster had planned for his sister instead.

Jonathan winced. He probably should have taken advantage of the darkness to cozy up to Phoebe. Would she fear he'd suddenly grown cold? As he'd walked away it occurred to him that he should have at least touched her, made plans to meet between her sheets again that night. But then Warminster had spotted his entrance and waved him over to his discussion. He couldn't have gone running to his lover without drawing unwanted attention to himself.

Besides, Phoebe was committed to a clandestine affair, and until he changed her mind he would do all in his power to let her have her way, but the truth wouldn't hide forever. With him sharing her bed, and planning to share it every night of this tedious house party, a servant was bound to gossip about the rumpled state of Phoebe's bed. Warminster might hear of their liaison well before Jonathan could break the news.

Lady Jocelyn tugged on his sleeve. "Don't you think so, my lord?"

The way she said 'my lord' set his teeth on edge. Although he'd previously found much to admire in Lady Jocelyn's flirtatious manner, Jonathan couldn't dredge up much enthusiasm for the chit anymore. Despite her fluttering lashes and encouraging hands, he had lost his enthusiasm for her completely. She appeared quite silly and indecisive. Two traits that irritated him immensely.

He hoped she could handle rejection because he quite frankly preferred Lady Warminster's company. Phoebe had an easy way about her, intelligent conversation, and a wicked sense of humor she tried valiantly to hide from everyone. The fact she let down her guard with him to reveal her true nature pleased him.

"I say, Selwood, are you at all with us?" Warminster stared at him with an odd expression, one eyebrow raised in query, amusement tugging his lips.

Jonathan dragged himself back to the moment. "Forgive me, I cannot seem to help wool-gathering tonight," he mumbled.

Warminster clapped a stunning blow to his shoulder. "Perhaps you should retire. We have a full day ahead of us tomorrow. Wouldn't want you to shoot a man and not the pigeons we're after, eh. I'll keep an eye on Miss Elizabeth for you."

Jonathan grinned. "Lizzy and Lady Warminster retired at the same moment."

"Oh, has she?" Warminster's jaw clenched.

Lady Jocelyn glanced at Warminster

sharply, a frown working over her features. She smiled suddenly, but it didn't seem sincere. "I'm sure we shall find ample amusements for the evening."

When Warminster smiled at Lady Jocelyn in return, Jonathan realized he'd cleared the field for his friend to have Lady Jocelyn's full attention. Well, good luck to him. He had far richer pastures to cultivate. "Goodnight then."

Jonathan spun on his heel and strode from the drawing room. It took some effort, but he managed *not* to run up the long flights of stairs leading to his bedchamber. When he had the door shut and locked behind his back, he collapsed against it. He ached to touch Lady Warminster again, so much so that his hands trembled as he stripped by moonlight, but he made sure his activities were loud enough to be heard in the next chamber. He wasn't quite sure if Phoebe would come to him again, yet he didn't want to test whether the door connecting their bedchamber's remained locked against him.

Last night it had been locked and he'd had to use the main door, risking discovery by Warminster or a guest. Tonight?

Jonathan ran a hand through his hair. Damn it all. He would never learn the truth if he didn't at least try. Slowly, he crossed the room until he stood before the solid oak door. The knob was cool to the touch. He tightened his grip and turned his wrist.

Unlocked.

A smile burst from his lips as the door glided open silently. He glanced into the darkness within. Had she left the door open willingly or merely forgotten to lock it against him? He took a pace into the room and stopped. Moonlight gave the chamber an eerie quality and he gulped at the deep silence. Was she even here at all?

He took another step, turning so he could see the bed fully. His pent breath rushed from his lungs. A lump lay under the covers and while he stared, Phoebe's legs shifted restlessly. He approached the wide bed, pulse pounding loud in his ears. She shifted again, sitting up as he neared and he crawled onto the bed to kiss her. His lady didn't resist him. She opened to him, letting him take her desire to mingle with his. Her hands plowed through his hair, tugging him tight against her as he teased her tongue, breathed her scent, and vowed to hear her beg for him before the night was through.

Phoebe fell to the mattress, dragging him with her as she went. He fumbled with the covers until their bare skin slid against each other. The hard points of her nipples grazed his chest, dragging a groan from her lungs. She was so tiny in comparison, small, delicate and soft where he was hard. Yet she clutched him with ravenous enjoyment, slid her fingers over his back and sides as she urged him to cover her with his body.

The temptation to plunder, to dominate, overwhelmed him, yet he wouldn't rush the moment. He hovered over her, keeping their hips apart while he kissed her as he'd wanted to all through dinner.

"You looked beautiful tonight," he whispered when their lips parted.

Phoebe skimmed her hand over his side, curling downward to capture his cock. "Thank you."

Jonathan grabbed her wandering hand and pressed it to the mattress. "What I really wanted to do was toss you up on the table before me, tug the gown below your breasts, and shape them with my hands." He pressed a quick kiss to her lips. "I'm told smooth polished wood feels wonderful against the skin. Have you ever made love upon a dining room table?"

She pressed her free hand over her face. "No," she squeaked.

He dragged her fingers to his mouth and pressed kisses to each knuckle. When he slipped them into his mouth and sucked,

Phoebe squirmed. He released them with a contented sign. "I'd love to see you spread over my dining table, legs wide as I sit between your thighs. You're all the meal I would want."

He fell to the mattress, lying on his side so he could touch his lover with ease. Her thigh slipped over his and he urged her closer by tickling between her legs.

Phoebe's hips thrust toward his hand, so he dug a little deeper, slicking his fingers in her abundant moisture. Her hips arched as he invaded. "Have you been teasing yourself without me here to watch you? Tsk, tsk. I might have to spank you for that."

She wrapped her hand around his cock and squeezed. "If you try to spank me I'll banish you from my bed." Phoebe began a lazy stroke, sliding her soft hand over him in maddening passes.

Jonathan inserted two fingers in her body and then slowly fucked her with them. When she was gasping, burying his fingers to increase her own pleasure he leaned close to her ear. "Many women get excited when they're spanked. Don't discount it until you try."

She tightened her grip. "You believe you're the only one skilled at seduction, don't you? Take your fingers out of me."

Reluctantly, Jonathan complied. He'd never

force his desires on a woman, and if she didn't like what he did then he'd certainly stop. When she moved and her hair skimmed his chest he gasped aloud.

Beautiful Lady Warminster, intelligent and highly aroused, climbed to her knees above him. As she pried his stiff length up from his belly and lowered her head to taste him, he anticipated soft kisses. His thickness prevented many women from taking him into their mouth, yet Phoebe persevered until she had his head nestled between her lips. The warmth from her wicked tongue as it skimmed over his skin dragged a gasp from him. Not many women wanted this, to pleasure a man so intimately. Yet the delighted hum, and fevered attention, proved Phoebe wasn't prudish in the least.

Jonathan settled against the pillows, pleased by the revelation. Given her adventurousness tonight, he wondered if there was anything she *wouldn't* do. With luck, and her agreement, they'd have plenty of time for experimentation.

Phoebe wriggled on her knees, swaying her bottom enticingly. Jonathan couldn't help but lay his palm over her skin and then raise it to deliver a stinging slap. Teeth clamped over his cock, not alarmingly firm, just hard enough to thicken him. He growled as he smoothed his palm over where he'd struck and when her jaw unclenched, he slapped her bottom again.

His cock popped from her mouth as she moaned. "Damn you."

Jonathan dragged her up his body so they touched from chest to thigh then widened her legs until she was open for him. "You liked that. Don't deny you are not wetter because of those slaps."

With a bit of juggling, he pressed the head of his cock to her opening, using his fingers to ease the way. Wet heat enveloped him as he nudged in an inch. Phoebe shuddered and then reared back, taking most of him into her with one smooth movement. The tight heat made his bollocks tingle, but he'd never wished for brighter light more. He wanted to see her bare skin, see his hands resting upon her thighs, and his cock invading her body.

Phoebe attempted to rise higher above him, but he didn't want to lose the connection to her skin. He rolled them to their sides, drawing her thigh over his. When he bent his head to capture her lips, she eagerly pushed her tongue into his mouth. Together they gripped and slipped, fucking slowly as they explored wherever they could reach. Jonathan massaged her rear. Phoebe had tensed. He waited for her to relax again before he smacked her delectable arse. She shuddered and pinched his nipples hard.

The unexpected pain took away his control. Jonathan slammed into her again and again, battering his way deeper, clutching her tight as the pleasure took over. Phoebe clawed at him until they were pasted together by their slick skin. He set his lips to the smooth curve of her throat and suckled as her fingers pierced the skin on his back.

When Phoebe's back arched, body tensing from a release that shook the bed, Jonathan followed, pumping his seed deep within her, losing himself in the bliss of perfect passion. She breathed raggedly as he raised his lips from her neck. Her hands caught and clutched his head, forcing his gaze to hers. "Don't you dare do that to me again. You might have killed me."

Jonathan raised a brow, amused by her reaction. "Nonsense. A little death never hurt anyone."

CHAPTER SEVEN

THE MIRROR DIDN'T LIE.

No matter how hard Phoebe peered into her looking glass, the evidence of her wickedness was right before her eyes, and before anyone else who glanced at her neck for that matter. She turned her head to stare at the incriminating imperfection on her skin. Selwood must have lost his mind completely to put her in such a position. She frowned as she skimmed her fingers over the mark. How was she to hide something so vivid?

She couldn't wear her hair down; that would cause no end of problems and draw notice. She could attempt to feign illness and remain in her room. But the bruise could take several days to fade and she couldn't hide forever.

She needed something to cover it. Phoebe

wrenched open her dresser drawer and fumbled through the contents. Lotions, perfumes, and sweet-scented soaps. But nothing to hide her problem. The door creaked and expecting her maid had returned, Phoebe rushed to draw her long hair forward over her shoulder, hiding the mark from prying eyes.

"Good morning, Phoebe, may I come in?"

She spun to find Lizzy Oliver, not her maid, inching into the room. Her face was pale, her gaze timid as she hovered by the door.

Concerned, Phoebe rushed forward. "Of course you may. Good morning."

"Is it?" Lizzy sagged so Phoebe quickly led her to the window seat and sat down beside her. She seemed exhausted.

Phoebe tucked a few stray strands of hair behind Lizzy's ear. "What troubles you?"

"Oh, everything." The younger woman folded over and wept into her hands. Astonished, Phoebe shifted to put her arm about her back, rubbing small circles as she cried. After a while Lizzy's tears stopped and she looked up sheepishly. "I'm sorry. I don't know what's wrong with me this week."

Phoebe smiled. Her emotions veered wildly this morning too, but she was not quite at the point of tears. If she couldn't find a way to hide the love-bite Selwood had placed on her neck, then she might very well consider it. She rubbed her hand over Lizzy's back once more. "I honestly don't mind. Do you want to talk about it?"

Lizzy sat up sniffing, appearing ready to wipe her eyes with her hands. Phoebe rushed to her dresser draw and pulled out a clean white handkerchief to give her. Once Lizzy was calmer, she leaned against the window frame for support. "Warminster is an arse."

Phoebe hugged Selwood's sister closer to her side. "I agree. He's positively beastly at times. I've found it best to ignore him."

Lizzy dropped her head to Phoebe's shoulder. "He thinks I should marry. He won't let the matter drop no matter what I say."

"Goodness, you must have been up with the crows to have already argued with him. I like to leave that dubious pleasure 'till later in the day. And after our discussion last night, I imagined you'd try to avoid him altogether by taking your breakfast in your bedchamber."

"I did have breakfast in my room. Early, as always. But Warminster slipped into my bedchamber and listed all of Lord Parker's sterling qualities."

"The list must have been very short." Phoebe stilled. "Wait. Did you just say Warminster was in your bedchamber this morning?"

Lizzy nodded weakly and then started crying again. Honestly, that man deserved a ball between his eyes for upsetting her friend so badly. No, wait. He deserved to be married.

Warminster had compromised Lizzy this morning.

It was just that no one had caught him.

God help him when I get my hands on him.

"Don't you even consider confronting him over it?" Lizzy whispered as if reading her mind. "I just want him to leave me in peace."

Phoebe set Lizzy a little apart, holding her by the shoulders until their gazes met. "What exactly did this morning's conversation entail?"

The younger woman peered down at her twisting fingers. "He woke me. Must have brought the housekeeper's key because I was sure I secured the lock. Said I should use the house party to get better acquainted with Lord Parker. He said he'd sing my praises while the men were out shooting this morning. He also suggested that I should put a little more effort into being agreeable." She shrugged. "I got angry. I got out of bed and tried to kick his feet out from under him again. Next thing I knew he'd dragged me to the floor with him. We struggled and he kissed me."

Fury rose up in Phoebe. If Warminster had seduced this girl in her own bedchamber this morning, she was going to find every pistol hidden in this house and put lots of little holes through his foppish hide. "What else?"

"Nothing whatsoever." Lizzy wiped her hands over her eyes furiously. "He left, slammed the door without a word. I was too stunned by his odd behavior to complain."

So, Warminster did have a bit of control, but to kiss Lizzy in such a circumstance? He must be out of his mind. Should she tell Selwood about this?

Lizzy sat up straight, breathing deeply. She slipped out of Phoebe's arms, but the struggle to remain calm was visible in the tense set of her shoulders. After a while, Lizzy glanced her way and offered a lopsided smile so much like Selwood's that her heart missed a beat. Phoebe returned it, holding out her hand to squeeze the young woman's cold fingers.

Lizzy's smile faded. "What is that?"

"What?"

"That mark on your neck?"

She had been so wrapped up in Lizzy's distress that she'd forgotten all about the lover's mark on her skin. She flicked hair over it. "It's nothing."

"It's not nothing." Lizzy's eyes widened. "Are you ill? Quick, lie down."

Lizzy reached for her again to peer at her

neck, but Phoebe did her best to evade. "I'm not at all unwell. It's a private matter, one I don't wish to discuss or have made public."

Unfortunately, Lizzy flinched at her sharp tone. Perhaps Phoebe should have softened her voice, but the shock of wearing such a telling mark on her skin had unsettled her.

"A real friend would tell me the truth." Lizzy's eyes filled with tears. "I should have known you were only feeling sorry for me. You cannot trust a Warminster to ever tell the truth."

"Lizzy, please, it's complicated."

"And I'm too simple to understand." Lizzy turned and rushed out the door.

Phoebe wanted to follow but, given her undressed state, she couldn't very well fly down the hall after her. Hastily, she shrugged out of her robe and nightgown, dragged a simple navy day dress from her closet and threw it over her head. Most of the buttons were hard to reach and while she fumbled behind her back, her bedchamber door burst open again.

Lizzy slapped her hand over the corner of a table, leaving a pot of something behind, and then rushed out again.

Startled, Phoebe drew closer to the object, discovering a cosmetic pot containing a beige cream fairly close to her skin color. Grateful for the unexpected gift, she hurried to the looking glass, slathered the contents over the mark until only a faint outline could be seen, and then rushed from the room.

Lizzy was not in her bedchamber, though all her possessions were. She was also nowhere on the first floor, or mingling with the guests on the ground floor. In fact, Lizzy was nowhere to be found.

By the time Lord Selwood returned with the shooting party an hour later, Phoebe was so distraught she feared she'd burst into tears. She rushed outside to meet him.

"I've lost Lizzy," she blurted out.

Selwood frowned and reached for her hands, drawing her away from the group of curious gentlemen. "Good grief, you're shaking. Have you really lost her or is she hiding? She used to do that as a child."

Despite the gawking gentlemen, Phoebe clutched at him. "She's gone from the house. I've searched and searched."

Jonathan shuffled his feet. "Perhaps she's simply gone for a stroll. She'll no doubt return soon."

Phoebe shook her head. "She was upset this morning and then we had a disagreement."

Selwood drew her to a bench and sat down close. "Tell me everything from the beginning."

So, she told him about Warminster's early

morning visit to Lizzy, holding Selwood's hand tight when her lover would have risen to search for the blackguard. She also mentioned Lizzy's discovery of the lover's mark on her neck. When she finished, Selwood appeared contrite.

"I lose all sense when we make love. My apologies."

"None of that matters right now. We have to find Lizzy."

He stood, held out his hand to draw her to her feet. His calm gaze settled her nerves. "That will be easy. Lizzy will have returned home to Dalemain Court." When he looped his arm about her shoulders and squeezed, Phoebe leaned into his chest. "Care to take a short drive to check on her? I shall deal with Warminster later."

Phoebe nodded, burrowing deeper into his warmth and dragged his musky scent into her lungs. As much as she'd jump at the chance to lead him upstairs again, she had to sort out the mess she'd made of the morning. Poor Lizzy. In her efforts to avoid scandal she'd inadvertently hurt a dear friend.

Selwood's arm slipped from her shoulder, but he captured her fingers and tugged. Together they strolled through the house, out the front door, and waited for a carriage to be brought round. Never once did Phoebe seriously consider dropping Selwood's hand. She needed the reassurance of his touch to prove he wasn't angry about how she'd handled his sister's questions. But most importantly, she hung onto him to prevent him from tracking down her stepson.

However, the sense of contentment that trickled through her as he handed her up into the carriage and settled against her side puzzled. Her lover was easy to be with, despite his much younger age. Lord Selwood, Jonathan, didn't rattle about like other young men. His calm, even temperament soothed where his older friend—Warminster—prickled and pinched. Jonathan projected an air of quiet reserve that hid his amorous inclinations very well indeed.

She shouldn't become used to being with him.

The short carriage ride was conducted in silence, but Jonathan constantly reminded her of his presence with the swipe of his thumb over the back of her hand. The gentle reassurance settled her heart and when the carriage ride ended, she calmly stepped out in his wake. He captured her hand again in a firm grip and led her into his rambling house, up the long flights of stairs and twisting corridors to Lizzy's bedchamber.

At the door, he knocked and when they heard no reply, Jonathan opened the door.

Lizzy huddled in a tight ball on the window seat.

Relief coursed through Phoebe in a rush and although she tried to loosen Jonathan's grip on her fingers, he pulled her all the way across the room with him. He positioned two chairs before the window seat and they sat to wait for Lizzy's acknowledgement.

When she didn't raise her head, he sat forward. "Shall I challenge him to a duel at dawn?"

"No."

"Did he frighten you?"

"No."

Jonathan dragged a hand through his hair. "*Ma petit*, I want so much to make things right."

"You cannot." Lizzy burst into another series of sobs that made Phoebe's heart ache. "Nothing is right anymore."

Cautiously, she got to her feet and sat beside the crying woman. When she didn't object, Phoebe scooted closer. Lizzy pushed her away.

"Do not be angry with Phoebe, little one. She is your friend and you know it."

Lizzy lifted her head and stared at her brother. "I used to believe so."

He winked at his sister. "Of course she is. Phoebe practically ran me down to tell me she couldn't find you anywhere at Moreton Hall. She's been looking for you for hours."

Lizzy turned to Phoebe but her gaze fell to her cosmetic covered neck. She swiped the beige paste away and held up her fingers for her brother to see. He stared at them then his grim gaze landed on Phoebe. By the tense set of his jaw, she guessed he wanted to set the matter straight with Lizzy, but because of Phoebe's own rules, she'd constrained him from doing so.

Heart pounding loud in her ears, Phoebe nodded, giving him permission to expose their affair, but she couldn't stay to hear how Lizzy reacted. She simply couldn't. "If you'll excuse me, I believe I will return to Moreton Hall where I belong."

Jonathan turned in his chair and captured her fingers again as she tried to escape the room. "Wait for me in my study. I'll escort you home myself."

Phoebe nodded and hurried for the hall.

CHAPTER EIGHT

"YOU GAVE PHOEBE QUITE A FRIGHT TODAY," Jonathan remarked as he settled beside his sister on the window seat Phoebe had just vacated. "I'd appreciate it if you didn't do that again."

Lizzy scowled as she wiped her damp nose. "I cannot believe you're defending her. I may not have understood completely this morning, but I have realized what that mark on her neck means now."

He leaned against the window frame. "Really. And that is?"

She appeared flustered by his question. "Oh, don't make me say it."

Amused, Jonathan leaned forward to rest his forearms on his thighs. "Well, if you're going to make accusations about a woman I hold in the greatest esteem, you'd better choose your words with care."

A shocked gasp left Lizzy's throat. "Did *you* make the mark on her throat?"

"I did." He shook his head. "A mistake on my part."

Beside him, Lizzy's breath rushed from her lungs loudly. After a long, silent moment, Jonathan turned to see her expression. His sister's mouth hung open then she snapped it closed and glanced about her. *So far so good.* At least she wasn't shrieking about him seducing her best friend. He glanced down at the floor while he waited for Lizzy to decide how she'd react to the revelation.

"A mistake? Did you not mean to make love to her?"

Jonathan chuckled. "Oh, I intended and accomplished that. My mistake was losing my head and failing to keep my end of the bargain. I appreciate you sharing your special cream. The lady has a reputation to maintain after all."

He didn't mean to sound despondent about that last condition, but he must have conveyed his disappointment too clearly because Lizzy leaned her head against his shoulder. "Those Warminsters are nothing but trouble."

Jonathan hugged her close. "I like Phoebe very much."

Lizzy squeezed him tighter. "Do you love her?"

While his head screamed *yes*, he wouldn't admit to something that utterly astonished him. He admired Phoebe, desired her so much he longed for her touch this minute. But love? He shook his head. "You mustn't entertain such fanciful notions."

Yet, he couldn't stop himself from entertaining the same now. Jonathan shook his head. "Now, what am I to do about Warminster? Shall I beat him to a pulp or slice him to ribbons on the field of honor?"

He watched Lizzy very carefully, but his bloodthirsty suggestions dragged a shudder from her. So, that was a *no* to any retribution. What could he do to make her feel better?

Lizzy sighed. "Back to you and Lady Warminster. What can I do to help you?"

Jonathan drew in a breath at the change of subject, but for now he'd allow it. "Nothing. Despite our affair, she will always be your friend. Forgive her for this morning, won't you? She was likely afraid you'd think less of her."

When he stood, Lizzy climbed to her feet too. "Thank you for coming to check on me. You really are a wonderful brother." She stood up on her toes and pressed a quick kiss to his cheek.

When she exited the room, Lizzy moved with customary haste. Jonathan stepped out into the hall, following her progress. What was going through her mind now? However, she disappeared down the servant's staircase without a backward glance before he could find out. Really, sometimes he wondered just what went on in her brain. He shrugged off his sisters' problems for now and took the stairs down toward his study.

Phoebe paced the room.

Jonathan took a moment to enjoy the view then he quietly locked the door behind his back. He must have made a sound because she turned to face him. The deathly pallor of her features hurried him across the room. "It's all right, *ma belle.*"

"I told you this was a mistake," Phoebe wailed against his chest. "How will she ever be able to speak at me again? I'll miss her so."

She broke into uncustomary sobs and Jonathan did his best to soothe her with his hands. The fact that she clung to him so readily made him feel ten feet tall. His sister's discovery of their affair had shifted the balance in his favor. With luck, he wouldn't do anything foolish again to further dampen the appeal of their liaison.

When Phoebe's sobs quieted, Jonathan swept her up into his arms and sat with her on his knee. She held to him. He could get used to this kind of afternoon more often. A pretty woman on his knee, quiet house about him.

A loud knock sounded on the door and they both jumped. Phoebe scrambled from his lap and put the entire room between them. He groaned as he climbed to his feet and unlocked the door. His housekeeper waited on the other side.

She cast a quick glance over his shoulder. "Lady Elizabeth suggested Lady Warminster might enjoy tea." She bustled past and set the tray on the corner of his desk, nodding politely to his lover. When she'd set everything to order, his housekeeper turned for the door and the impish grin on her features startled him. She winked as she swept out the door.

Damn that Lizzy! She'd told the servants.

When he looked up, Phoebe appeared confused. "Lizzy cannot be too angry with you. She sent tea." Jonathan relocked the door, skirted the desk and sat down to read the small stack of correspondence that had built up over the past few days. After a few minutes, Phoebe moved to sit on the other side of his desk to pour her cup of tea.

"There isn't a second cup. Should I call your housekeeper back?"

Jonathan snorted. "I hate tea."

Her brow wrinkled. "You take tea whenever you come to Moreton Hall."

He winked, but he turned his attention to the correspondence rather than explain himself. Phoebe was a clever woman. Eventually, she would work it out.

"Oh," she whispered.

Jonathan let her absorb his odd past behavior a while before he spoke. "How do you like Lord and Lady Parsons? We have an invitation to a soiree in three weeks' time."

Phoebe's cup rattled to the saucer. "They are a well-placed family. Their daughter is coming out soon."

"Hmm, this ball must be for the daughter then. What are her chances of making a good match?"

"Quite good. She's a beauty." Phoebe's voice wavered with her admission.

"Ah," Jonathan murmured then set the letter to one side. He picked up the next. "And what of Lord Prescott? I'm invited for a week-long shooting party next month."

"His daughter is a sweetheart," Phoebe whispered. "Very kind."

"Right." Jonathan dropped the invitation with the other and continued through the pile. He had a lot of invitations from families with eligible young daughters. And by the end of the short stack, Phoebe looked profoundly uncomfortable. "What are you doing for the next few months?"

She appeared surprised by his question. "I'll be here, of course."

"Hmm," Jonathan grumbled. *So, no rendezvous away from these parts.* Disappointing.

He dragged out parchment and wrote out the brief replies. He sealed his letters with a heavy sigh and rang the bell for his butler. Once the notes were dispatched to his servant's care, Jonathan returned to sit on the edge of the table near Phoebe.

"So," she began. "You're off to Dorset next month. I'm sure you'll have a wonderful time." Phoebe offered him a hesitant smile, settled her empty teacup to the tray, and then pressed her palms to her thighs.

"Well, no, actually." Jonathan settled his hands to his hips. "I sent my apologies to all of them." He wasn't going anywhere without her. At least, not yet.

Again she appeared startled, so he leaned forward to capture her lips. After a brief, intoxicating kiss Phoebe pulled away. "The door?"

Jonathan curled his hand around her skull

and pulled her to him. "Locked," he whispered against her lips and then kissed her again.

The intense heat of her mouth drove him wild. He pressed her deeper into the chair, falling to his knees until he burrowed his hips between her thighs. When the material prevented him from getting closer, he impatiently scooped up the dark blue muslin until he could touch her skin.

Jonathan ate at her mouth, rejoicing when her tongue tangled with his in a heated dance. She threaded her fingers through his hair and kept him close, deepening the kiss until their teeth grazed. He hooked his fingers under her thighs and tugged her bottom toward the edge of the chair. Impatiently, he bumped his already firm cock against her sex.

She whimpered and squirmed to put a distance between them. "No, Jonathan. Not here," she moaned. "Your sister and all the staff are in the house, probably outside the door."

"Then it will teach them to eavesdrop on us." He dragged her against him, firmer than before. "This is my house and I want to make love to you here where I spend my days. I want to inhale the scent of our lovemaking while I read my newspaper. I want to remember the image of you spread over my desk as I fill you up."

Jonathan picked her up off the seat and settled her bottom on the sturdy partner desk. With one swipe, he cleared the surface of blotter, teacup, and the unlit candelabra.

She gasped at the noise. "Jonathan, we shouldn't."

Before Phoebe could say another denying word over his intentions, he kissed her, lavishing her mouth in a furious assault on her senses. He palmed her knee, inching her closer to the edge, and to his body. Her other foot curled around his thigh, unconsciously encouraging as he dragged her the remaining distance until her heat pressed against his length. Frantically, he snapped his jacket from his shoulders, ripped open his trousers, and shoved the long fold of linen from his shirt up under his waistcoat out of the way.

She fell to her elbows, gasping. "This is madness."

But her eyes fell to his rigid length, prodding against her damp curls. Jonathan thickened further at the sight. "And you love it. Admit it?"

He took himself in hand and swiped the head of his cock through her dampness. Phoebe squirmed, legs parting to accommodate him. He propped himself over her body, holding himself away so only the tip of his cock touched her skin. After several passes over her rigid nub, she squirmed closer.

Jonathan didn't give her what she wanted. Although it pained him, he shifted away an inch. Her gaze flew to his. "Admit what you want, Phoebe, and then I will pleasure you 'till you scream."

She curled her hands about his neck and tugged, hard, persistent. When he didn't bend all the way to her waiting lips, she growled. Actually growled. If he didn't need to hear the words so badly, hear her say she desired him, he might have laughed.

As it was, he was in no hurry to end this interlude. He could restrain his passion until she gave him some encouragement of her own.

Phoebe licked her lips, glancing toward the door. "Come closer."

He complied, but with a quick shift of her hips the movement settled his cockhead at her entrance. She tightened her legs about his thighs. Jonathan resisted her entrapment and waited.

She licked her lips again. "All right. All right. I desire you," she whispered, glancing at him shyly and then quickly lowering her lashes.

"To do what, exactly?" he whispered.

Phoebe dug her fingers deep into his shirt-covered arms. "I desire you to push that beautiful cock of yours inside me."

Jonathan invaded a little and then stopped.

She panted impatiently. "All the way."

He pressed forward slowly until he reached her limit and stopped again.

Phoebe tossed her head then reached to capture his hair to pull his lips close to hers. "If you don't make love to me properly, Jonathan Oliver, I will spank your perfectly round arse until it's red. Move," she ordered.

Pleasantly surprised his gambit had paid off, Jonathan did as he was told. He let his instincts take over as he made love to her, smooth strokes gliding into the intense heat of her passage. Beneath him, Phoebe breathed raggedly on every thrust. The sight of her wild abandon, her hair falling from her combs to lie over his mahogany desk, quickened the movement of his hips.

But he wasn't anywhere near close enough. He caught up one of her legs, and stretched the shapely flesh over his arm, altering her position until her body opened wide. The greater depth, the slick flesh rubbing against his engorged cock, slowed his pace. He wanted to savor these moments of pleasure with her. He wanted to imprint her passion on his soul.

Jonathan caught her gaze as he slipped his fingers over her nub. She gasped again, hips rising to push her flesh harder against his fingers. While he held her gaze, he stroked over her with sure flicks of his fingers, delighting in her efforts to suppress the sound of her enjoyment. Her glazed expression told him she was very close to finding release. He kept his thrusts hard, slow, until her back arched from the desk and a strangled scream erupted from her throat. Jonathan rode out her contractions, gritting his teeth over the need to come too. When she subsided, legs falling away from their tight grip on his body, he withdrew and took himself in hand.

The slick, hot length slid easily over his palm, setting every nerve he possessed alight. Phoebe's eyes fluttered open and then she glanced down to where his hand stoked over his engorged flesh in a slow rhythm. She rose to her elbows as he shoved her gown higher up her hips, pushing the material aside until he could see the smooth white expanse of her belly.

He tightened his grip, fisted himself quicker as her eyes widened. Phoebe's leg tightened its grip around his thigh, bringing him closer. "Ah, hell, Phoebe. The sight of you lying like that is going to torture me for the rest of my life."

Desire raced up his spine, his body stiffened then shuddered as his seed shot over her belly, marking her perfect skin with the evidence of his desire. His brand.

Once the last spurt landed on her skin, Jonathan fell to the desk, using his hands to keep his weight suspended. Phoebe blinked up at him and then another shy smile, the kind filled with warmth and affection lifted the corners of her mouth. He leaned in to press a hard, possessive kiss to her lips.

CHAPTER NINE

IN ALL HONESTY, Phoebe should be considerably alarmed by her willingness to skirt scandal with her lover. She had let him, no begged him, to make love to her over his wide study desk. Twice. She pressed her hands to her flaming cheeks and kept her gaze fixed outside the carriage window. Thank heaven no one seemed in the mood to make conversation during the return to Moreton Hall. She couldn't utter a coherent word that wouldn't sound strained.

The mark on her skin was sufficiently covered again with another application of Lizzy's special cream. To her surprise, Lizzy's skin near the base of her neck sported an angry red mark Phoebe had never noticed before. She had reluctantly revealed the imperfection, explaining how she had hidden it under clothes until she'd matured then started applying the cream to her skin so people wouldn't whisper that she was ill. It was a birthmark she'd been born with apparently, not an actual illness.

Her attention turned to the occupant of the carriage. Jonathan sat across from her, relaxed and more handsome than any gentleman should be allowed. His gaze was already fixed on her, his lips curled into a warm smile. Despite the presence of his sister, she quaked in response to the wicked gleam in his eyes.

What had happened between them had tumbled her world into shambles. Her lover affected her with just a look, a touch, and a deviously worded invitation to make love to him. Oh, the things Jonathan Oliver did to her senses defied description. However would she bear the loss of such attention when the affair ended?

And it had to end. Warminster must never learn of her indiscretions with his best friend, although, her stepson was doing a fine job of damaging his own friendship with Jonathan by kissing Lizzy.

Beside her, Lizzy Oliver sat with a smug smile hovering on her lips.

Little minx.

The woman should be scandalized to have a

friend debauched in her home, yet Lizzy seemed more than willing to return home with Phoebe to keep up the pretext that they had been together the whole time. Lizzy would have to know Phoebe had just made love to her brother. Neither of them had been able to restrain their enjoyment to make the encounters quiet ones. Half the servants would be whispering too. She just hoped they might be inclined to keep their master's secrets.

Again, her gaze fell on Jonathan as the carriage turned 'round the drive. But he sat stiffly now, jaw clenched tight.

Phoebe leaned forward and laid a hand on his knee. "What is it?"

"Warminster is on the front steps. Waiting."

At Lizzy's sharp gasp, Phoebe captured the other woman's hand. "Please, Jonathan. Do not lose your head and challenge him. You must consider your sister's reputation."

His frown deepened. "That might be the only reason the bastard has legs left to prance about on his front lawn with." Jonathan covered her clutching fingers under his broad palm and squeezed. "I'll deal with him once this wretched house party is over. Never fear."

When the carriage drew to a halt, Jonathan climbed out first. From where Phoebe sat, she could tell the two friends had locked gazes, but couldn't tell who was winning the battle of wills. However, it was Warminster who glanced at the carriage first, noticing her presence and Lizzy beyond. Jonathan snorted and held out his hand to Phoebe.

As their palms connected, a tremor passed through her. This might be the only time they would touch for the next several hours. The thought of that distressed her. She liked his possessive hands on her skin. When her feet hit the gravel, she turned to wait for Lizzy.

The young woman came to her immediately, twining their arms together tight, ignoring Warminster completely. Her stepson took a step in their direction, but Jonathan moved between. Considering it wise to take the source of tension far away from trouble, Phoebe pulled Lizzy with her. She clearly needed some help where Warminster was concerned.

Resolved to be a better friend, she led Lizzy into the house, passing Warminster so she stood between them. When they crossed the threshold, neither looked to see how he took the cut. The manor was quiet about them as she swiftly dragged the younger woman up the staircase and along to her room. Most of the guests must be elsewhere or resting up for the dinner and games tonight.

Once the door closed behind their backs, Lizzy expelled a harsh breath. "Pompous idiot. Did he intend to intimidate me?"

Phoebe leaned against the bedpost. "Lizzy, do you have any idea why Warminster is so keen to marry you off? It's not like him to meddle outside his own family party."

The other woman shrugged and moved to the window. "Perhaps he doesn't like his advice to be ignored. I told him to mind his own business on the first day of the house party. He's been hounding me ever since."

That wasn't like Warminster at all. Phoebe had the distinct feeling she was missing an essential piece of information that would explain why their association had reached boiling point so quickly. But she couldn't very well press the woman to share the confidence. Lizzy might expect Phoebe to be equally forthcoming about her liaison with her brother, and she wasn't in any way sure how to classify that.

Phoebe moved to the window too. "Ah, the archery contest is over." She peered at the raucous group approaching the house. Lagging behind the rest, with a tall gentleman leading her way, Lady Jocelyn sauntered daintily across the lawn. Warminster and Jonathan strode out to meet them. From her vantage point, Phoebe had an unimpeded view of their tête-à-tête.

Lady Jocelyn flirted shamelessly, fluttering her fan to encourage the gentlemen. When Jonathan took a step back from the group, Phoebe let out her breath. She hoped that meant Jonathan was disinterested in Lady Jocelyn. She really hoped that was true.

"I'd wager Lady Jocelyn has won handily at the archery," Lizzy mused. "She looks too well-satisfied to have not had success."

"Lady Jocelyn has other interests on her mind right now." Phoebe turned from the window. "She's currently trying to encourage both Warminster and Jonathan into offering marriage. Her mother confided this to me last night."

"That despicable harridan! Last night she had Warminster and Mr. Perkins trailing after her like hungry puppies. How many gentlemen does she need?"

"More than a few, I fear." She shrugged. "None of them have proposed marriage yet."

"Warminster has an empty-headed ninny as a candidate for his wife?" Lizzy threw up her hands. "Oh, of course he does."

When Lizzy started pacing, Phoebe settled comfortably to watch. In all honesty, Lizzy should not be disconcerted by Lady Jocelyn's designs for marital bliss. Yet, she realized something had changed in her friend's manner. Instead of appearing amused by Lady Jocelyn's ambitions, she seemed jealous. Just what exactly had happened between her and Warminster?

Lizzy crossed to her wardrobe and threw open the door. "What should I wear this evening?"

With the change in conversation, the afternoon progressed smoothly. Phoebe chatted and helped her prepare for the evening and then they both retired to her room. While she dressed for the arduous dinner ahead, Phoebe tried to ignore the bumps and thumps from the room beside hers. Jonathan's loud conversation with his valet pricked her ears, yet with his sister hovering she couldn't slip into his room to capture even a brief kiss.

Besides, nothing they ever did was brief. Every conversation, touch, and decadent pleasure seemed to soak up hours not minutes of time. In Jonathan's company the world disappeared, yet tonight she wouldn't be so lucky.

Once she was as ready as ever, Lizzy captured her arm again as they strolled downstairs to the drawing room where everyone would be gathered.

A few steps past Jonathan's bedchamber door, he joined them. "No disappearing without me tonight. Understood?"

Phoebe wasn't sure whether the man meant her or his sister, but she nodded anyway. She would soak up every second she could until their affair ended. And after that she'd consider what she had done.

Jonathan breathed a sigh of relief as the ladies left the men to their port. After an endless dinner of polite conversation, he wanted to wipe the fraudulent smile off his face. Lady Jocelyn had placed her hand to his arm so often that the couple sitting opposite had begun to cast speculative glances at them. She'd dominated the conversation too, filling in the silence and speaking for him when he'd offered no opinion. That last had annoyed him. She didn't understand the first thing about his opinions, but he hadn't liked to embarrass her in front of everybody. He may no longer want her, but he didn't wish her ill. Besides, she'd possibly end up married to his best friend so they needed to get along.

To his considerable disappointment, Phoebe had been placed too far away for easy conversation. She'd stayed with his sister all afternoon, and while he didn't begrudge their friendship, he was necessarily forced to stay away. Even though his sister approved of their affair, he hadn't wanted Phoebe to be discomforted. Besides, he suspected he hadn't the power to keep his hands under control if he had set foot in her bedchamber.

"A penny for them, Selwood." Warminster plunked a bottle of brandy on the table between them and sat in the opposite seat.

"Nothing remarkable. I was just considering the shooting expedition tomorrow. Should I take my Brown Bess or my dueling pistols? Both have remarkably light triggers."

Warminster appeared a little startled by the talk of dueling, but Jonathan let the satisfaction of seeing him squirm deflect some of his irritation. Warminster could have the Clifford chit for his wife while Jonathan had Phoebe in his bed. But Warminster had better leave Lizzy alone. If he caught wind of any more private conversations he would shoot him.

When the port and cigars were consumed and smoked, they rejoined the ladies.

Lady Jocelyn looked set to approach him. She smoothed her gown, set her features with a welcoming smile, but he veered left to join Phoebe and Lizzy on a sofa.

When he was comfortable, Jonathan leaned close to Phoebe's ear. "Miss me?"

He couldn't hover, and she didn't utter a

word in reply, but she didn't hold herself as stiffly as she had. Or perhaps she was just afraid he'd come to blows with Warminster over port. Either way, the lady cared about him and that made him the happiest man in the room.

Jonathan reclined in his chair and let the women's conversation flow over him. They were talking about the ladies excursion tomorrow and planning a detour into the village. How well they got on together. They laughed and giggled in the coziest fashion that one tended to find only among the fastest of friendships.

And he thought he might just love her, if this feeling of giddy happiness was any indication. Given their interactions during the day, and last night, he wanted to explore what might grow between them. He wanted to wake beside her for certain, make love whenever they could. If he chose Phoebe for his wife, and not another young lady, Lizzy would be very happy too.

Besides, Phoebe didn't belong here at Moreton Hall. Warminster had always kept her to the side of the family party, discouraging her from feeling at home here once he'd taken on the burdens of the title. Jonathan had tried hard to control his fury over the shoddy treatment, but was glad when Phoebe had struck up a friendship with his sister and visited their home often. As much as Lizzy had blossomed under

Phoebe's calm presence, that friendship granted him the added bonus of seeing her frequently. They'd become friends, but he hadn't been lucky enough to get her alone for any length of time.

Not until Warminster had handed him the opportunity he needed on a silver platter.

The tantalizing idea of marriage to Phoebe made him impatient. He had come to this house party with that specific aim in mind. Only his heart had led him to choose a different woman, one more experienced and better suited to his temperament. Thank God for his impulsive heart.

Phoebe glanced at him, her pale gaze quizzical. With a heavy sigh, he forced himself to sit still until the party broke up. And it should have appeared to all that his leaving just happened to coincide with Phoebe and Lizzy's departure. It wasn't, of course. Once Lizzy was secure in her bedchamber for the night, he followed Phoebe down the hall. But instead of entering his bedchamber through his door, he slipped through Phoebe's, too impatient to wait another minute to take her into his arms.

As always, Phoebe welcomed him, drawing him firm against her with as much passion as he. Impatiently, he shredded the clothes from her body and his, popping buttons across the floor until they were both naked, both frantic to become one. As they fell to the mattress, Jonathan made a vow that before the night was over he'd tell her he loved her, and that he wanted so much more than these brief decadent nights.

CHAPTER TEN

JONATHAN SWIPED a long strand of hair away from his nose, rolled, and drew the soft body sharing his bed closer to his chest. Well, not exactly *his* bed. Although the sun shone bright through the windows he was still firmly entrenched in Phoebe's wide tester, but he refused to creep away before she woke. It was nice here, cozy without the world looking down upon them. Contentment trickled through him as he dragged in a deep breath of sex-laden air.

His body thickened at the memory of the previous night's pleasure. How had Phoebe survived without sexual intimacy before sharing her bed with him? The lady's appetite rivaled his, and he simply couldn't keep his hands off her delicious curves. Jonathan let his fingers slide over the smooth flesh of her hip. She shud-

dered, hands spreading over his chest unconsciously.

The reaction brought a smile to his face.
Even in sleep she clung to him. What he
wouldn't give to stay with her forever. He prac-
ticed the phrases in his head that he wanted to
utter when she woke. He wanted his proposal to
be perfect so she would say yes straightaway.

They could have the banns called and
marry in three weeks. After that, he wondered
if she'd enjoy a wedding tour to Brighton. But
all he really needed was to know she was his
to touch and protect and love. A solid, well-
made bed like this one wouldn't go astray
either.

Jonathan glanced up at her bedchamber
ceiling, feeling more comfortable here than in
his own guest room. No doubt the presence of
Phoebe made him feel so at home. She shifted,
her breasts brushed his chest and a ragged sigh
passed her lips. Intrigued, he inched back a bit
to see her face.

She slept still, but if he were not mistaken
she dreamed.

Her body grew restless against him, hips
arching toward his. Slowly, careful not to waken
her, he inserted his leg between hers. Phoebe's
thighs clamped around his leg and her sex
pressed against his skin. Amused, he decided to

see how far his lady could go in her fantasies before she wakened.

He urged her with his hands, sliding her sex against his firm thigh until he grew slick with her desire. She woke with a gasp, blinked, and then glanced up at him guiltily. "Good morning."

Phoebe dipped her head to his chest. "Good morning."

Feeling altogether too excited to let the moment pass, Jonathan rocked her against his thigh again. "Were you having a wicked dream?"

"Oh no," she whispered.

He flipped her about so her back snuggled into his chest, prodding her sex with his cock. Instinctively, she settled his cockhead into place and he pressed into her tight heat. Ignoring the urge to thrust hard and deep, he set about increasing her pleasure. He slipped one hand over her sex, the other cupped her full breast. A satisfied moan left her lips. Jonathan nudged into her, keeping the movements calm, building her arousal higher.

She seemed impatient with his slow loving because she rocked her hips against him eagerly. But he kept her passion under his control, making love in the manner he'd begun, sliding his fingers over her sex and her nipples. When he pinched, she buried her face into the pillow.

Her moans and gasps grew louder and louder around the muffling pillow until she tensed and appeared to strangle as her release overtook her.

Jonathan straightened her hair from around her face and he turned her head so she had to see him. Her dazed expression and rapid pant brought another smile to his lips. He'd definitely take her in the mornings when they married.

Biting his lip to hold in the urge to propose right that very minute, he slid clinging strands of hair from her brow and pressed a lingering kiss to her cheek. The taste of her sweat damp skin on his lips heightened his arousal so he thrust again.

A loud bang on the wall made them both jump.

Jonathan glanced at the door that connected Phoebe's bedchamber with his as a male voice rose in anger.

Cautiously, Jonathan slipped from Phoebe's body and bed to stare at the connecting door. Yes, he had remembered to lock it, but something definitely odd was happening in his bedchamber. That room should have been locked from the inside. No one should be in there.

"I'll kill Selwood for this." Warminster threatened from the next room.

A female voice cried out piteously in answer and Jonathan glanced at Phoebe only to find her skin white with shock. She stumbled from the bed and reached for her nightgown and wrapper, throwing them on carelessly in her rush. When her beautiful skin was covered respectably, she tiptoed to the door and pressed her ear to it.

Just as quietly, Jonathan reached for his breeches and slipped them over his hips, pushing his softening member into the tight confines. Unfortunately, in their haste to make love last night there were buttons missing from the garment and they wouldn't stay on properly. That could be embarrassing should it be discovered. He snagged his shirt from beneath the bed and threw it over his head. The long linen would hide the state of his breeches, but what could he do to hide himself should Warminster decide to include Phoebe in whatever drama was happening next door?

He glanced toward his lover and found her backing away from the door. She glanced at him and then frantically waved her hands in the direction of the bed. Did she want him in it or under it?

Under it, he decided, as she snatched up his cravat, stockings and boots and shoved them into the nearest drawer. Jonathan fell to the floor and scrambled under the solid bed. He moved until he hid in the exact center and then the world grew dark as Phoebe straightened the bedding so no one could see him beneath. He watched the pink tips of her toes move about him and then she disappeared from sight.

Phoebe's heart beat so loud she feared she might faint. Next door, Warminster was ranting about Lady Jocelyn sleeping with Jonathan, and very soon everyone in the house would suspect that something was seriously amiss. She had to take steps to stop this disaster. She couldn't let Warminster convict his best friend of such a scandalous act when he'd been with her instead.

Frantically, she straightened her tumbled hair into some semblance of decorum and approached the connecting door. Taking a deep breath, she turned the key and knob and stepped into the fray.

Lady Jocelyn sat on Jonathan's rumpled bed, sheets pulled up to her chest, defiance clear on her face. Her shoulders were bare.

Phoebe's stepson appeared without his usual disguise. There was none of his usual foppish charm or elegance on display.

"What do you want," Warminster snapped. "This is none of your concern."

Phoebe stepped close to him. "Get yourself under control now," she whispered urgently. Warminster blinked and met her gaze. She tried to convey how out of character his behavior seemed without saying so out loud. She tightened her wrapper. "Well, you woke me and your discussion appeared diverting. What a shame it's all foolish nonsense." She turned for the bed. "Your bedchamber is on the other end of the hall, Lady Jocelyn, as you well know. Was there something the matter with your accommodations?"

The glance Lady Jocelyn sent her was triumphant. "This room has been very welcoming to me. Unlike some I could name."

Warminster winced. "I explained I had urgent business to attend to."

Lady Jocelyn scowled. "At night? Every night of the house party? I swear Warminster, you are toying with my affections for your own amusement. Well, I won't stand for it. Lord Selwood appreciates me and is desperately in love."

Phoebe choked. She'd never imagined Lady Jocelyn would have the nerve to behave like this. Attempting to entrap a lord, or any man, into marriage was fraught with all kinds of danger. What if they refused? What if a duel was fought for her honor and someone was killed?

What if society shunned her even if she married?

Lady Jocelyn hopped off the bed, bold as brass in an obscenely revealing shift, snatched up her wrapper and threw it over her shoulders as she strolled out the bedchamber door. Phoebe hurried to shut it before turning back to her enraged stepson.

"Where the hell is the bastard?" Warminster's voice still had a hard edge and his hands sat on his hips in a threatening stance. "Clifford will kill him for this."

"I suggest you lower your voice, Warminster, unless you want everyone to question where you've been at night because I believe I have a fair idea. I heard about yesterday morning's interlude in another bedchamber in this house. I've done my best to distract Jonathan from any murderous tendencies, but I'm still surprised he hasn't filled you with shot holes already."

"Nothing happened." Warminster moved forward, leaving her uncomfortably close to her stepson, a place she never liked to be.

Phoebe pushed at his chest. "Jonathan did not rendezvous with that chit. He isn't even here. The walls are thin. I would have heard something before you barged into the room. I heard nothing at all through the night."

Warminster glanced about him, distaste on his features. "Then where is he to clear his name? By now every servant in the place would have discovered that Lady Jocelyn met with him."

"Only because you pranced in here like a bull in a china shop and believed her."

Warminster crossed his arms over his chest. "Why are you defending the degenerate so staunchly? He seduced an innocent."

"Oh, for pity's sake," Phoebe hissed. "He didn't do anything of the sort. Lady Jocelyn has been flirting with the pair of you at the same time. But apparently you haven't been attentive enough so she planned this little scandal to secure a titled husband. Either one of you would do for her. However, you must have neglected to fall at her feet often enough."

Warminster scowled. "I wouldn't put myself out for any woman."

"Yes, I can actually believe that." Furious that Warminster was so dense, she had little choice but to reveal Jonathan's location. "Come this way."

Phoebe spun about and walked into her own bedchamber. After a moment or two, Warminster followed. "What?"

"Shut the door."

Warminster raised an eyebrow but did as he

was bid. The slam of the heavy door raised goose bumps along her arm. Was it really wise to share such a confined space with a spy who could probably kill you without compunction?

Taking a deep breath for strength, she set her hands to her hips. "Jonathan, come out!"

There was a low scrape then Jonathan's head popped out from under the bed. "Thanks, it's a bit dusty under there, better tell Warminster that his servants..." His voice trailed off as he noticed Warminster's presence across the bed. The two friends stared at each other, belligerence on both faces.

"When today is over . . ." Warminster growled.

". . . we will have a very long, private discussion about your behavior toward my innocent sister," Jonathan finished.

Warminster's hands curled into fists. "You planned to punish me by seducing Lady Jocelyn. I intended to offer for her."

Jonathan crossed his arms over his rumpled shirt. "Seducing her would be punishment for me. She's definitely not worth the trouble."

"No. How dare you deny it? I found her in your bed."

"Technically, yes, you found Lady Jocelyn there and I'll not deny that. But I was not with her," Jonathan said.

"No, not when I found you. Did you attempt to hide in here from me?"

"Not at any time." Jonathan's jaw clenched. "I didn't run in here to hide. I didn't sleep in my bedchamber last night. Just like you apparently haven't been doing for the duration of the party. If you had then you'd be the one finding Lady Jocelyn in his bed."

"Then where did you sleep?" He folded his arms across his chest, his expression growing obstinate. "Go on, this ought to be good."

Jonathan's gaze fell on her and he swallowed hard. At this point, it seemed Warminster was incapable of believing anything different unless they laid out the cold hard truth before him.

Phoebe nodded and closed her eyes. She didn't want to see Warminster's disgust. She'd had enough of the man's prickly disposition to last her a lifetime.

Jonathan crossed the room and set his hand to the small of Phoebe's back. "I slept in Lady Warminster's bed tonight, and last night."

Silence thickened around her, and she opened her eyes to see Warminster's reaction to her scandalous behavior.

The smirk on Warminster's face showed he didn't believe Jonathan. Not one word of it. As she stared at her stepson, Phoebe accepted she might have no choice but to save Jonathan from his own friend's blindness. She rubbed a shaking hand across her brow, waiting for a miracle. When none came soon enough for her liking, she moved closer to her lover.

"Jonathan did sleep here all night, Warminster. And the night before that too."

Her lover curled his fingers over her hip and she took comfort in his steady presence. Her stepson turned to face her, disbelief clear in his expression. The knowledge he considered her so unappealing rattled her calm.

Incensed, Phoebe punched Warminster's arm. "Oh, for Gods sake, must you be so entirely dense? What do you imagine Jonathan might be doing in my bed all night? It certainly wasn't lace making."

CHAPTER ELEVEN

"YOU MUST BE JOKING." Warminster laughed outright at the news Phoebe and Jonathan were lovers.

Apparently, Jonathan didn't care for that reaction either. His arm tightened around Phoebe's waist as he pulled her to his side. "No. You know me better than to imagine I'd lie about something like this. It is the truth," he warned.

Nervously, Phoebe glanced up. His jaw was set in a stubborn line as he stared at his amused friend. She set her hands to his arms where they wrapped about her waist and pushed.

Despite her attempts, Jonathan wouldn't release her. His breath beat against her cheek. "Let me fix this, my love."

Across the room, Warminster wiped his eyes, still chuckling. He still didn't believe them. Gradually, when neither of them joined in his merriment, he appeared to absorb their words. He flickered his gaze over Jonathan's protective stance, her rumpled state, and then behind them. A sneer curled his lip as he gestured toward the neatly made bed. "Nice try."

Jonathan set his head alongside Phoebe's, snuggling her tighter against him and inhaled deep. "Is he always this dense?"

The blush that crossed her face must have lit the room at Jonathan's open display of affection. Not even her late husband had behaved so casually before his son.

Phoebe glanced up again, lips colliding with the rough stubble of Jonathan's jaw. "Yes. I'm afraid so. Do you believe we need to go so far as to complete the act so he might pay attention?"

The warmth and desire in Jonathan's gaze set her heart to tumbling down a long well of pent up dreams. He made her experience sensations she had no right to expect at her age. But then again, Jonathan had always made her want. She accepted the quick press of lips to her temple and attempted not to blush harder.

"I hope not," he whispered, seduction in his tone, the hard ridge of his erection pressing impatiently into her bottom again. "The man can find his own amusements. And apparently has. Something we will need to discuss soon."

When Jonathan snuggled Phoebe into his arms so they both faced Warminster as a couple, she could swear her stepson's eyes would fall from his head. "Dear God. Are you mad? She's *old!*"

Phoebe dropped her gaze to the floor, embarrassed by Warminster's accurate assessment of Jonathan's state of mind. He should want a young woman in his arms, not someone past her prime. He shouldn't desire someone so much older than himself. Feeling the chill of discomfort cover her skin, she briskly rubbed her arms.

Behind her back, Jonathan tensed. "I would suggest you watch your words, Warminster. Any cut you deliver to Phoebe is a direct cut to me. I will not stand by and listen to you disparage her."

Warminster took a pace away from them. He pushed his fingers through his hair, disturbing the elaborate pale curls in a way he usually wouldn't dare. But his reaction to this affair was very telling. Everyone would be surprised. Scandalized.

Hoping the worst was over, Phoebe squared her shoulders. "The situation between Jonathan and myself is irrelevant to anything but Lady Jocelyn's accusation. If it becomes necessary, I will speak up on Jonathan's behalf against the girl."

The connecting door flew open again as Lizzy stormed through. "I should say so. The whole house knows of her behavior by the way." She skirted Warminster as if avoiding a deadly cobra and stopped before her. "Good morning. What an abominable mess."

Lizzy pressed a kiss to her cheek and turned on Warminster. "Go. Go deal with Clifford properly, Warminster. She's making a bloody spectacle of herself."

He blinked. "Get the hell away from those pair. Do you realize what they've gone and done?"

Lizzy glanced down at her fingers, appearing disinterested in Warminster's violent protest. "Of course. I'm not as foolish as some people I could name. Oh, dash it all. I've broken a nail."

Whatever discomfort Lizzy had experienced yesterday had apparently passed. She seemed more than capable of handling Warminster now. Phoebe had never had a champion before. The novelty was quite singular.

Warminster growled and grasped at her arm. "Come away."

With a quick blur of movement, Lizzy had Warminster flat on his back, gasping in pain from the hard fall to the timber floor. She stood over him, arms tensed for a fight. "I told you not to touch me again, you scoundrel. I don't need your hands on me, and I certainly don't need to listen to the stupidity you spout. Go and deal with Clifford before she makes it impossible to show her face again. Oh, and just so you know, I'm perfectly happy with this arrangement. Jonathan has loved Phoebe forever. You're blind not to have known."

Phoebe gasped in shock at Lizzy's blunt pronouncement. He couldn't love her. She was far too old for that.

Behind her, Jonathan tensed and his hold tightened.

Warminster crawled to his feet, groaning. "Should have remembered you were fond of that trick," he muttered, hands held out before him to ward off Lizzy should she try again. He glanced at them again, a frown creasing his face. "Told you to watch over her—not seduce her, Selwood." With a shrug, he ended the discussion, turned on his heel, and stalked from the room.

"Well, thank goodness the pretty boy has gone. We have a lot to do today," Lizzy said. "Jonathan, kindly release Phoebe so we may prepare to go into town. I'm looking forward to escaping Moreton Hall for some fun with my friend. Thank heavens this is the last day to suffer through this gabbling crowd."

Jonathan dropped his head to Phoebe's shoulder. "Nothing kills a man's passions like the arrival of family. I should get dressed."

Phoebe smiled at the disappointment in his tone. Like her, he really did appear to enjoy the physical aspects of their affair. A pity tonight would be the last night of such close and constant loving. She set a hand to his jaw. "Probably for the best. There will be enough babble among the guests to make them wonder at your absence. You'd best go clear the air about last night."

"I certainly will." Jonathan pressed a lingering kiss to her lips. Warmth, lured by the expectation of further pleasure, bubbled inside her, desperate for fulfillment.

Reluctantly, she moved her head away. "Good luck with the hunt."

His smile deepened then he strode out of her bedchamber without another word.

Unfortunately for Phoebe, she missed him as soon as she couldn't see him. And given that their early morning tryst had been interrupted, he'd walked away unfulfilled. She'd have to make it up to him tonight. The thought of surprising him brought a smile to her lips.

Lizzy cleared her throat. "Really, I see you love and adore him, but could you possibly wait 'till I'm gone before you smile like that again," she urged. "I might love you, and the idea of you and my brother, but I'd rather have no inkling of what you plan to do with him when you're alone again." She wrinkled her nose and crossed to the wardrobe.

Oh dear. Did Lizzy imagine their affair a grand love match between equals? But the only thing equal would be the depths of their passion. Jonathan quite easily stole her ability to behave as a respectable widow should. However, with yet another person aware of her scandalous liaison with a gentleman ten years her junior, Phoebe couldn't really claim any respectability.

Jonathan couldn't love a woman who'd fallen so far from grace as she had this past week, never mind that he'd taken her there himself. At her age, she should have acted with some semblance of intelligence. How foolish to blindly accept a lover into her bed.

Feeling the heavy weight of the world settle on her shoulders, Phoebe dressed. She chose a dark silk, simple, modest and fitting for a woman of her elevated years. Although Lizzy bounded by her side during their shopping expedition, the threat of future scandal depressed her spirits.

"I say Phoebe, are you at all listening to me?"

"Sorry, Lizzy, my mind is elsewhere this morning," Phoebe murmured as she held up a long length of deep green ribbon against Lizzy's hair. "How about this one?"

Lizzy shuddered. "No thank you. I believe Warminster has a suit of clothes in that exact same shade."

"Warminster has more clothes than most ladies," she replied briskly. "It's impossible not to match him in some way."

"That doesn't mean I shouldn't try. How is it that you can stand him? The man is so incredibly stupid. I mean, just consider the idiots he invited for this party. I've not heard a sensible word from one of them all week."

"Lizzy," Phoebe began carefully. Should she set the girl straight about Warminster's other, secret activities? Lizzy could be incensed to find out that Warminster had hidden his true nature behind that of a fop all her life. But hadn't this foolishness gone on long enough? Given everything that had happened recently, she didn't have a choice. It was simply too dangerous for Lizzy to goad a man so capable of killing her if he was incensed enough and lost his head. "Not everyone behaves honestly at these affairs. Warminster doesn't believe half the notions he prattles on about. It's a well-staged act."

"An act?" Lizzy returned the green ribbon to the pile and scowled.

"Yes, a performance. Like a masquerade or a farce. You've been to a play where the characters look one way but act another. You should not always believe what you see at first glance. Especially with Warminster."

Lizzy's fingers curled into the pile of ribbons and she methodically straightened them. She didn't raise her head and didn't speak, so Phoebe continued to browse, thinking Lizzy hadn't paid attention. Besides, she had to consider her future beyond tomorrow. After Warminster's guests departed, she should cut all ties to Jonathan and do her best to forget that she'd ever been so indiscreet as to take her stepson's friend as her lover. Perhaps she should move to another of Warminster's properties, a distant one to keep temptation at bay. He should like to have her out from under his nose, once and for all.

Yes, that sounded like a grand plan.

But she would also be leaving Lizzy behind. That thought truly saddened her. She had grown used to Lizzy's friendship, her coltish ways as she moved about. How sad to think that she might never see her again. Or be here to witness her marry someone special. And the young woman deserved happiness with a man that would adore her.

All of a sudden, Lizzy's head snapped up. Her eyes widened and then her lips curled into a smile so unlike her usual expression. Alarmed, Phoebe returned to her side and clasped Lizzy's hot fingers.

When Lizzy's smile fell upon her, Phoebe wondered perhaps if the young woman had grown mad. The calculating expression on her features frightened. Lizzy patted her hand. "Warminster has played his last game."

"Lizzy?" Phoebe tugged on her fingers, trying to separate herself from her friend. She didn't like that expression, didn't like the way her eyes had lit up with glee.

Lizzy laughed, chuckling in her usual fashion. "Oh, Phoebe, I'm going to make that ridiculous popinjay regret ever pulling the wool over my eyes. And I'm going to have a damn fine time doing it. Let's return to Moreton Hall. We both have a gentleman to torture." She threw whatever she'd been looking at to the shelf and spun on her heel.

When Phoebe couldn't see her anymore, she quickly paid for her items and hurried outside. Her friend had already settled into the carriage, fingers drumming against her knee impatiently. "Lizzy," she whispered. "You are not going to expose Warminster are you? Believe me, despite the foolish charm, he's not a man to cross."

Lizzy folded her arms under her breasts. "Oh, I know that. Now. Thanks to you. But the bounder does need to be taken down a peg or two. Trust me; I'll be content to see him get his comeuppance in privacy."

Despite Lizzy's threat against her stepson, Phoebe's thoughts turned inward. It would be beyond embarrassing if word of her affair with Jonathan spread beyond her control. When Moreton Hall came into view, she steeled herself to betray nothing but calm. Yet guests lingered about the vestibule, buzzing like bees around honey. Were they there because of Lady Jocelyn's behavior or had they learned that she had seduced a younger man?

Phoebe wasn't sure, but when Lady Clifford spotted her, the scowl that crossed her face made her quake. As the whispers grew to a dull roar, she tried to ignore the sense of panic. Thankfully, Lizzy captured her arm in a tight grip and guided her up the stairs before she could blurt out something incriminating.

CHAPTER TWELVE

"WHAT ON EARTH WERE YOU THINKING?" Warminster chided, as they stalked through the long grass after their fallen quarry.

"I had a clear shot at it." Jonathan bent to pick up their prize. The poor bird was a bit battered and bloodied since both men had shot it at once, but the important thing was he had fired first. Not bad for a civilian against a spy.

He handed the bird off to the waiting servant.

"That will be all for today," Warminster told the man as he handed over his rifle and gestured for Jonathan to do the same. Reluctantly, Jonathan parted with his weapon. A faint stir of disquiet thrummed though him at the conversation to come. He'd been waiting all morning.

Warminster turned and scowled. "Lord and Lady Clifford plan to leave this morning, but I cannot guarantee they won't blacken your name over this."

Jonathan grunted. "They can try." He didn't particularly care about the conniving little chit. He only cared for Warminster's reaction to him and Phoebe. Could they remain friends?

"She still claims she shared your bed last night."

He chuckled. "Couldn't have, I've been too busy seducing your stepmother."

"About that." Warminster toed a tuft of grass. "I am surprised at you."

The midday sun beat down on his head as he considered how to answer. "I love her. I've loved her since I first laid eyes on her. Remember, you used to tease me that I'd turn into her lapdog if she snapped her fingers."

"You were young, and she my new mother."

Jonathan shrugged. "My admiration hasn't dimmed as I've gotten older. When you warned me of her plans that first night at the ball, I decided to act before she changed her mind."

Warminster scratched a hand through his hair. "Still can't believe she'd do it—seduce her son's best friend."

"Actually, it was the other way round."

Jonathan grinned impishly. "Perhaps I've been around you too long, but the lady didn't realize I spent the night in her bed until the next day. I loved her in darkness, using my best French to do it too."

Warminster's mouth fell open. After perhaps a minute, he snapped it closed. "Yes, I remembered you saying the ladies loved that once. And when she discovered the truth?"

"I received the reaction I expected."

Warminster winced. But sympathy wasn't required. After the initial shock had worn off, he'd lured Phoebe in his arms again and again since then. But he needed to clear the way to keep her there.

"I want to marry her, Warminster. I want your blessing."

His friend appeared shocked. "An affair is one thing, but marriage? What if she is incapable of providing you with an heir? My father never came close to siring one with her."

"I was not terribly surprised she didn't conceive given your father's nature and your mother's circle of male friends." Jonathan tilted his head to one side, considering his friend's possible reaction to his next words. Warminster fidgeted. "I figured it out, why all the paintings of your father disappeared into the attic on his death. You don't take after him at all, do you?"

Warminster's jaw clenched tight. After a very long moment he turned his head to stare at his friend. "No."

"Don't get your hackles up." Jonathan clapped him on the shoulder. "It's quite common. I do remember the painting from the morning room where we used to meet so often. He was about your age in that if I remember correctly."

Warminster let out a deep sigh. "Should have known you'd notice. But will you treat my stepmother any better than he did if she doesn't reproduce?"

Annoyed his friend thought him so shallow, Jonathan crossed his arms over his chest. "I have accepted the possibility, but I love her enough that it simply doesn't matter. Your own mother, through design or accident, found a way to produce the needed heir, but not a second son. Phoebe had more morals than to cuckold her husband to do it. I admire her highly for resisting the temptation to please the bastard."

"Lady Warminster is unusually high minded."

Jonathan let his arms drop. "Was that a compliment?"

Warminster picked at some grass seeds stuck to his sleeve. "I've never said I hated the woman. Just didn't care for her snooping about."

He sighed. "Besides, it's better that the world at large thinks us at odds. Far safer for her given my line of occupation."

"She'll be safe with me."

"Well, one less to worry over." Warminster glanced up at the cloudy sky. "She fooled me. The Clifford chit fooled me. Damn it, I'm slipping."

For a man in the spy trade that could be a very bad thing to believe. He relied upon his instincts to survive. Cautiously, so as not to startle, Jonathan set his hand to Warminster's shoulder and squeezed. "Perhaps you should consider a change of career, my friend?"

Another sigh rattled out of Warminster's chest and Jonathan dropped his arm. "I must admit, the thrill of the chase has lost its allure of late. The most fun I've had this last year is when you joined me in Paris."

Unlike Warminster, Jonathan remembered those few days with horror. They'd been hiding from their pursuers in every low place imaginable. Desperate, hungry beyond words, and without a single credential to prove them English should they be intercepted by either French or English forces save for impeccable accents in both. After that nightmare assignment, Jonathan had declined further involvement. "You need a partner."

"A partner?" Warminster's frown deepened as he gazed off into the distance. He drew in a deep breath, let it out slowly, and turned to meet Jonathan's gaze. "Perhaps. I'll consider it. The trouble will be convincing the right one."

"I'm sure you can be persuasive. I take it you have someone in mind?"

"Yes, perhaps I do." A sudden grin broke over Warminster's face, a smile reminiscent of simpler times. "Come. We should return to the Hall and clean up. We have guests to entertain."

Since all was settled between them for Jonathan to propose to Phoebe, the trek to Moreton Hall was conducted in friendly silence. Once Warminster had disappeared from sight, Jonathan wandered to his bedchamber door, opened it, and slipped inside. Empty.

Thank God.

Wearily, he rang the bell. After trekking through the woods all day he was ripe enough to repel even himself, but he wanted everything to be perfect for tonight when he proposed. Fantasies and fears for the future brought alternate smiles and frowns to his face over the course of his bath.

They would be happy together. He was determined to put her first before all other concerns, yet there was still a very real fear in him Phoebe would reject him in favor of maintaining her respectability. She was much too concerned about the gap in their ages, and hers being on the high side of his. He hoped he'd done a good enough job of making her last rule inconvenient to her.

Dressed and refreshed to face the evening gathering, Jonathan strolled down the main staircase and along to the billiard room. He received some odd looks from the few gentlemen in the chamber, but they kept to themselves and their game.

He poured himself a drink.

"I'll have one too, Selwood," Warminster requested as he swept into the room. Jonathan poured it and then turned. The glass slipped through his fingers a bit. He tightened his grip and crossed to his friend.

Warminster had outdone himself on this last day. Pearl encrusted waistcoat, buckles on his shoes. The brilliant white satin blinded. No one could possibly take him seriously after this. While the man entertained his guests, jovially dragging Jonathan into the group and proving that the morning's gossip wholly unsubstantiated. Jonathan laughed along with the jokes, but his mind stayed fixed on Phoebe until they were summoned for dinner.

Unfortunately tonight, Warminster had

placed him further along the table than he'd like, and he only occasionally caught Phoebe's eye. He sat between Lady Weston and Lady Beecham, two of the elder guests in attendance who gossiped around his head as if he wasn't there. When the dinner ended, they all trooped toward the ballroom to await the local guests.

He seized the moment to pull Phoebe from the room, and out into the moonlit garden. "I thought that meal would never end," he whispered as he curled his arm around her waist to draw her deeper into the shadows of a large tree.

"Warminster must entertain lavishly." She wriggled against him provocatively, encouraging his hands to travel her back and then swoop low.

"I missed you today."

Instead of answering, his lover turned, captured his face between her palms and drew his head down. The first touch of their lips pulled a contented sigh from her, so Jonathan set about pleasuring her mouth. As usual, Phoebe clung to him, and then wound her arms tight about his neck, pressing against the thickening length of his erection.

He broke the kiss and buried his face in the crook of her neck. They swayed like that for quite some time, and then he moved her so her back was to the tree and captured her fingers. She never wore rings. The smooth skin was unmarked by any man's gift. "I had a pretty speech prepared for this moment, but the long and somewhat flowery words seem to have frozen on my tongue. Marry me, Phoebe. Say yes and be my bride."

She tugged her fingers from his grip. "No!" She moved away from the tree and him before he could recapture her fingers. "Absolutely not!"

No matter how hard he'd prepared himself, her outraged refusal cut. "What is so wrong with the idea of marriage to me? You would be adored, included in my whole life, not pushed to the side with no consideration as you are now."

As Phoebe backed further away, nervously glancing left and right, his temper rose. "*Good enough to fuck, but not good enough to be seen with as an equal.* Are you embarrassed of what we have shared? My feelings cannot come as too big a shock. I'm in love with you. Can you not understand that?"

She violently shook her head. "It's just lust. Nothing more. A man your age shouldn't tie himself to an old woman."

Jonathan cut off her words with a sharp

hand movement. "Enough about your age. You are a beautiful intelligent woman. Can you not see the numbers are meaningless where there is love?"

"I never said I loved you," she whispered.

His heart stopped. She didn't love him? Not even a little?

As she fidgeted, his unease grew. He had poured all his love into those stolen moments, determined to show her how much he cared. She hadn't allowed anything else. He should have realized his affection wasn't returned by the furtive way she had kept him to their burgeoning relationship. Jonathan looked away, insides curling in knots.

"I am sorry, Jonathan. I never meant to mislead you about the future, but you belong with someone much younger."

Pain unbearably tightened his chest. He forced air into his lungs, blinking rapidly to clear his vision.

Phoebe stepped closer. "Jonathan?"

"Do you imagine I'll be happy with someone like the Clifford chit? They're all like that. Never a care for the man, only after a title to elevate them in society." Jonathan curled his hands into fists as he fought to contain his emotions. "Madam, I suggest you return to the house. Someone might wonder where you are.

We simply can't have that can we, Lady Warminster?"

At that, his composure threatened to break. He strode away, around the house and off into the night without a backward glance for his fractured future.

CHAPTER THIRTEEN

A DULL ACHE had spread to every part of Phoebe's body, draining the last of her composure away. Her gloomy chamber mocked her with its emptiness and tantalizing memories of delicious pleasure.

Daybreak was lightening the horizon, but at a snail's pace to ensure she suffered enough. She welcomed the discomfort because she deserved every bit of pain for what she'd done to Jonathan. He'd wanted far more than possible. He'd wanted everything and more. Yet in time he would learn a young man deserved better than a barren old woman to wed.

He deserved someone unafraid to love him in return.

Phoebe turned her gaze to the gardens, not really appreciating the view. The maze was wreathed in clinging shadows, making it seem sinister and evil to her eye. At least the maze held no memories of Jonathan. Perhaps she'd be able to go there to forget the memories of his determined seduction—a seduction that had claimed her heart.

She'd lied to him, of course.

In truth, that was the only choice she had. Although the pain of denying her love for him had twisted her insides in knots, a clean break would set him free and in time he'd forget all about her. But she wouldn't forget him.

The sound of movement carried from the next room.

Phoebe's breath caught at the creaks and bumps from the adjoining bedchamber. Her spine stiffened. Last night she hadn't dared crawl into bed to sleep the night alone. The pristine bedding mocked her as she sat where she'd rested since she'd stumbled into the room, wounded by her own decision to refuse Jonathan's astonishing offer of marriage.

But there was no rest possible on this horrible morning because in a few short hours, minutes perhaps, he would leave his bedchamber and she would quite likely never see him again.

During the night she'd made the decision to leave Moreton Hall.

Although her plan was more cowardly than kind, he would be spared any further discomfort of meeting with her again. Perhaps he would appreciate that she took herself away, yet her relocation would spare her pain too.

In the next room Jonathan moved about restlessly, and the ache of longing pricked her conscience. She'd wounded them both last night in order to save herself later. Any woman he married needed to supply him with an heir. And for a brief moment yesterday she'd dreamed conceiving might be possible.

Yet, she'd never birthed or even come close to carrying a child in the six years of her marriage. And it was not as if her husband hadn't attended her bed often enough. Five years of such constant attention should have been ample to make her belly swell. But in the sixth year, when the nursery finery had been returned to the attic, Warminster had shunned her bed, resigned to her barren state. The memories of those horrid last months, when he'd turned elsewhere for his pleasure had returned to haunt her last night. How cruel men could be when thwarted.

The walls rattled with the slamming of a door and then the chamber next door fell silent. Panicked that Jonathan moved further away, Phoebe stood on shaky legs. But a disturbance within the maze caught her eye and she turned to see two figures running for the house.

Curious, she pressed her hand to the hazy glass to determine which furtive lovers they might be.

Her mind could not believe the sight at all. It stuck fast on the absurdity and drove away her pain. The gentleman in white silk glowed bright against the dark garden, the woman blended in with her dark green gown. But there was no mistaking her coltish tendencies as she kept pace with Warminster. There was no possibility of misunderstanding the young woman's clinging regard as they disappeared from sight beneath her window either.

Lizzy and Warminster!

Phoebe pressed her hand to her mouth to cover a moan.

She closed her eyes and saw those smiling faces once more in her mind, turned to each other with joy. Pain sliced through her chest. Jealousy beat at her composure. So Lizzy would get a husband after all. But Warminster's gaudy manners and form at her side for all to see was not what Lizzy had originally planned. She was brave to take him on, much braver than Phoebe had ever been. She pushed the envy aside, embarrassed that she could be jealous of her friend's happiness. She'd chosen her path herself, a life of her own choosing. She'd make her own rules.

For the first time ever she was free to make her own choices.

Determined to cease her wallowing, Phoebe snatched open a drawer, hunting for fresh clothes for the day. Instead, she found Jonathan's cravat where she'd hidden it just yesterday, before the mischief Lady Jocelyn had tried to create.

Hands shaking, breath churning erratically, she lifted the linen to her face. That scent, clean, warm and distinctly Jonathan brought her pain rushing back.

She wasn't free at all.

She fell to her knees in agony just as footsteps rumbled beyond her doors. Servants, by the sound, coming for his things to speed his return to Dalemain Court. She held the cravat tight to her chest, rocking on her knees as his trunks were collected and taken away.

After the silence of long minutes, a tear trailed down her cheek. Determined not to appear any more foolish for weeping on her knees, Phoebe clambered to her feet before her maid found her sitting in this dramatic, foolhardy way.

So she'd had rules for taking a lover? Jonathan had met all with ease. Clean, experienced, discreet and not averse to a clandestine tryst. Yet, that last one niggled because she'd been proud to be on his arm. Was it really so bad to be adored by a younger man? Was it unforgivable to find what might be true love after all this time?

***

"So, this is quite a surprise," Jonathan replied, trying his best to appear happy. Before him stood his sister and his best friend, Warminster, each slightly rumpled with small twigs and leaves stuck to their hair.

"With your permission, we'd like to marry. I've convinced Elizabeth it must be St. George's Church and no where else." He lifted Lizzy's knuckles to his lips and pressed a lingering kiss there. "I want the whole world to see who captured me and encouraged me into more sober habits. By the way, I'm retiring."

His infatuated smile and declaration turned the knife in Jonathan's heart. He wanted so much to be happy for them, yet his own disappointment dampened his reactions. His face ached with the strain to smile. "Congratulations again."

Lizzy peered at him, probably wondering at his awkward flat tone. To conceal his pain, he gathered her in his arms and hugged her tight, hiding his face and hopefully conveying without words his consent for the match.

"*Je vous remercie beaucoup, frère.*"

"*Juste être heureux, enfant,*" he whispered in return.

When he let her go, Warminster quickly recaptured her attention, carefully plucking out the small leaf matter from her hair and pressing them into Lizzy's palm with a laugh. Jonathan turned his back on their obvious affection, breathless with the need to scream out his agony.

A door creaked behind him, but he didn't need to turn to see who entered. Lizzy's delighted shriek to Phoebe stilled his heart. He willed himself to turn, to join the merriment and ignore the pain of Phoebe's refusal to love him in return. His feet wouldn't move. He took steadying breaths as yet more voices joined in congratulating the happy couple, the noise of the conversations rising steadily. Phoebe sounded happy over the engagement. Far happier than he. A knot of cold dread swept over his skin. Would she laugh off his declaration of love now as if it mattered little? He couldn't bear that and, knowing he must, he spun on the spot to face the room. And her.

But Phoebe was already watching him, standing between him and the house guests crammed into Warminster's study to gawk at the newly betrothed couple. He curled his fingers into tight fists as she approached and despite his best intentions, he drank in her presence.

The dark, demure gown and severe coiffure didn't dampen her affect on his senses. When she drew close, he inhaled sharply to imprint her scent on his soul, noticing as he did the dark circles beneath her eyes. She lifted her hands to his chest, and then slid them slowly upward toward his shoulders. She rose to her toes, lifting so their faces were closer, and he instinctively caught her hips to steady her.

The small gasp she uttered skimmed across his lips and he swallowed at the tension between them, the tightening of every pore as desire licked up his spine.

"I lied," she whispered, and then pressed her lips tight together.

Jonathan's heart clattered in his chest as he brushed his thumbs over her waist. Hope, that foolish emotion, gripped him. "Why?"

"Afraid," Phoebe whispered as her gaze dropped. "You'll cast me aside one day for someone more youthful. My husband flaunted his mistress before me when I failed to conceive. It hurt."

Surprised by that bit of information, by the

cruelty her husband had inflicted by not loving Phoebe as she deserved, he drew her closer, forcing her to take one more step into his arms.

Slowly, he spread his fingers over her back, cradling her tight against him. "Perhaps I should be afraid that someday you might replace me with a younger man, one with more stamina than a bull. I'll get old too. And the men in my family have a sad tendency to lose their hair."

As he'd hoped, a small laugh escaped her over his last confession, breaking the tension altogether. A mischievous smile lifted her lips. "Well then, I'd better enjoy my hold while I can —seeing as how it's merely temporary."

Like the sun rising on the horizon, Phoebe rose again to capture his lips, hands sliding through his hair, nails scratching across his skull to hold his head close for her kisses. His heart that just moments before had felt battered and bruised relaxed as she claimed him before witnesses, pronouncing an end to their discreet liaison.

"Should I plan for a double wedding, Selwood?" Warminster asked cheekily.

Wild applause drowned out Jonathan's less than friendly response.

The End

WILD RANDALLS SERIES

Engaging the Enemy ~ Forsaking the Prize
Guarding the Spoils ~ Hunting the Hero

*

SAINTS AND SINNERS SERIES

The Duke and I ~ A Gentleman's Vow
An Earl of Her Own ~ The Lady Tamed

*

REBEL HEARTS SERIES

The Wedding Affair ~ An Affair of Honor
The Christmas Affair ~ An Affair so Right

*

MISS MAYHEM SERIES

Miss Watson's First Scandal

Miss George's Second Chance

Miss Radley's Third Dare

Miss Merton's Last Hope

ABOUT THE AUTHOR

USA Today Bestselling Author Heather Boyd believes every character she creates deserves their own happily-ever-after—no matter how much trouble she puts them through. With that goal in mind, she writes steamy romances that skirt the boundaries of propriety to keep readers enthralled until the wee hours of the morning. Heather has published over fifty regency romance novels and shorter works full of daring seductions and distinguished rogues. She lives north of Sydney, Australia, with her trio of rogues and a four-legged overlord.

Learn more about Heather at:
Heather-Boyd.com

www.ingramcontent.com/pod-product-compliance
Lightning Source LLC
Chambersburg PA
CBHW031022190726
48286CB00003BA/973